ACCOLADES FOR PREVIOUS WORK

AMERICAN BADASS

—*American Badass* contains a story like no other. Zombies, Vegas, and a group of diverse characters, what more can you ask for in a fictional story? Taking what could be a very dark and glum story, the author adds just enough flair of humor that the book sucks you in and holds on to you tightly with its zombie grip and you don't struggle or try to run, you just keep flipping through the pages until you reach the end or do you? BRAINS!

—I don't really know what to say about this book except for the fact that I laughed. I laughed a lot. When the author took his protagonist, a zombie, to Las Vegas then the fun really began. I can think of only one other episode of a mythological beast being placed in this city of sin that hit home as well as this story and that was Chrisopher Moore's Coyote Blue. It was a party with zombie who had morals. It gave wonderful insight into the absurdity of pop culture, our over-obsession with violence, and most importantly, what it means to be human. And through all of this it made me laugh. Did I mention that it made me laugh? Because it was a funny book.

50 SHADES OF BRAIN

—Sequels are sometimes a disappointment. Not this one! Hilarious, full of excellent riffs on pop culture and geeky nerddom (I'm a citizen), and a truly remarkable gift for colorful language. Excuse me, wangwage. I hope the author has more stories to tell. This and *American Badass* are going on the same shelf with my Myth Adventures and Bill the Galactic Hero collection.

—I absolutely love Chacon's American Bad ass books. I'm already anticipating the third book in this series...If you love zombie books and haven't read these then GO READ THEM NOW.

—With evil Elvis impersonators and an extended riff on *The Princess Bride*, this book is hilarious.

E-MALE: OF MOUSE AND MEN

—I have been taking this book with me everywhere I go, so I can dip into it for a refreshing break. As a woman, I appreciate this peek into the friendship between two men. They have an excellent sense of humor. When they are on a roll, be prepared for smiles, chuckles, and laughter. If you want to brighten your day, get this book.

—A close friend who I correspond with primarily via "e-mail" sent "E-Male" to me and said "You must read this!! We are Fe-Male!" As a confirmed literature snob (Give me Pynchon or give me death Yes, some could argue there is no difference), I would have tragically overlooked it. Instead, I read the book cover to cover, unable to separate myself from it until its conclusion. Rarely have I been so amused and touched by such fresh, honest, direct, unique, yet eerily familiar voices. While I grew up in a completely different world from Anthony and Jeff, I felt an instant connection. This book is a timeless anthem to the Generation "X" pilgrims. While it is remarkably clever and hilarious at times (the unwavering focus on the men's friendship and lives remains brilliantly subtle), these delicate layers of friendship, marriage, career and maturity must be properly appreciated or the essence of the book is utterly lost. What makes this book particularly precious is that some people just won't "get it."

FLOOD

Published in the United States by Wooden Stake Press, LLC
Denver, CO
www.woodenstakepress.com

ISBN 978-1-940936-21-5

Cover and book design by Stewart A. Williams

FLOOD

JEFF CHACON

WOODEN STAKE PRESS

All he wants to do is fish
all he wants to do is fish
don't have a home
don't have a name
he don't know fortune and
he don't know fame...

—The Replacements

INTRO

Depending on your intellectual leanings, Heaven might be defined as one of the following:

A) A sumptuous place featuring barely-imaginable earthly delights. Unlimited Netflix. No jobs. Fast cars, top-flight champagne, top-flight clothes, and top-flight caviar, all crammed into top-flight palatial estates, one for each lucky and/or well-behaved person who made it to Heaven A. All within walking distance of a mall and a liquor store.

B) A chill place, featuring an existence of extended bliss, where each lucky and/or well-behaved person who made it to Heaven B floats around on clouds all day (after morning yoga) and marvels at the wonders of the universe. Within floating distance of a mall and a liquor store, of course.

C) A place where nothing, nothing ever happens. If you're a big fan of the Talking Heads.

D) Or perhaps Heaven is more utilitarian than A, B or C, more functional. With hierarchy and structure and spreadsheets and printers that don't work and comparative market analysis and crappy coffee and office parks where bland celestial middle management teams meet semi-regularly in bland celestial conference rooms to keep the bland celestial machine fed, to keep it all going, to carry out the orders of the Creator. An accountant's dream, an artist's hell.

Heaven D is where our story starts. Six months ago. On a Monday.

SCENE 1: IN THE BEGINNING

Six Months Ago. Monday.

O pen Mic Mondays at the Celestial Coffee Shop ('Home of the Stars!') were a music lover's heaven. Literally and figuratively. Elvis Presley hosted, Jimi Hendrix was a regular, and Prince, Buddy Holly, and Kurt Cobain traded licks as Keith Moon kept the backbeat and Phil Lynott laid down the funky bottom. The assemblage of unparalleled talent produced an unequaled cacophony of uniquely combustible auditory sensations.

And then there was Steve Easdale, a lamb in a room full of lions.

On Open Mic Mondays, Steve sat at the back of the stage with his paisley Fender Telecaster and tried to keep up, an endeavor ripe with uneven amounts of success. Like all of Steve's endeavors. As you'll soon find out.

And on this Open Mic Monday, Steve was supposed to be somewhere else. Steve was supposed to be at a bland celestial

meeting with a bland celestial middle management team in a bland celestial conference room; compared to jamming with Elvis, Jimi, Prince, Buddy and Kurt, bland timeliness felt unimportant. To Steve.

Besides, the band was about halfway through a thirty-seven minute jam on "Purple Rain" and Steve wanted to see it through, so he could see how Prince played the crazy solo at the end of the song. And then, Steve promised himself, he would go to the bland celestial meeting. He could be a bit late, right?

Right?

Wrong.

"So what's this all-hands meeting all about?" Bill Fofill asked, from his high-backed pleather-bound celestial conference room chair. If he were an occupant of earth, he would have been a middle-aged Southerner, with an eye for big trucks and little government. "I have target practice in an hour."

"I don't know," Linda Fablinda replied from her own high-backed pleather-bound conference room chair, seated across the white melamine conference table from Bill. She was a lithe brunette, tall in stature, with little room in her existence for nonsense. "The Amicable Representatives of Kismet have not met in damn near two thousand years. That's a long time between meetings, even for us."

"What does that mean, anyway?" Bill asked. "'Amicable Representatives of Kismet.' Such big words. So mysterious. I've always wondered."

"It means that we're representatives of fate or fortune, Bill."

"Well, we must be important – they told me to cancel the earthquake I was planning today!"

"Another quake, huh? Where were you going with this one?"

"California."

"Oh."

"Does that bother you?" Bill asked.

"Was it going to affect Los Angeles at all?"

"Centered in L.A, of course. Where else would it be?" He looked at the room around him. White walls, white ceiling, white board, white conference table...this room could really use a stuffed animal head on the wall, he thought to himself. He turned to Linda. "Wait, why do you ask?"

"I was planning a series of riots for L.A. today. And stale peanut butter and banana sandwiches. Not like these." Linda reached over to a bite-size-sandwich-filled white plastic plate on the table and picked one up. "Yummy!" she said, eyeing it with good intent.

"Really?"

"Yeah," she replied, after swallowing the sandwich whole. "But two acts on the same day? Isn't that much?"

"Well, it's Los Angeles. What do you expect?"

A young woman in a sun dress, a flower blooming from her waist-length blonde hair, entered the room. 'Sunflower,' her name tag said.

"Hi everybody," she said, as she sat in a high-backed pleather-bound conference room chair next to Bill.

"Hi, Sunflower," Bill said.

"Soooooooooo, what are we doing here?" Sunflower said.

"That's what we're trying to figure out," Bill replied, his voice a drawl that wouldn't be out of place on a wild turkey shoot.

"Well, whatever it is," Sunflower said, her voice a soft lilt that wouldn't be out of place teaching nude yoga inside a hot canvas tent, "it's good for the city of Los Angeles."

"What do you mean?" Linda asked, her voice a commanding presence that wouldn't be out of place running an international conglomerate.

"Well, I was about to hit them with mudslides and really bad traffic," Sunflower replied.

"Wow," Bill said. "Don't they already have really bad traffic?"

"So on the same day," Linda said, like she was numbering points on a PowerPoint presentation, "Los Angeles was going to see an earthquake, riots, mudslides, and really bad traffic? And stale peanut butter and banana sandwiches? Have their numbers been bad lately? Or what?"

"Last time I checked," Bill said, picking his teeth with a camouflage toothpick, "their numbers were down in the dumps."

"Maybe this meeting was set up by the City of Los Angeles to prevent us from destroying the City of Los Angeles," Sunflower replied. For a moment Bill thought he saw an elk hiding behind the flowers on her dress and he wished he had his rifle. Stupid gun-free celestial conference room.

"Or, hell," he said, "maybe we're going to be ordered to just destroy the crowded dump once and for all." He made a gun with his hand and pointed it the wall. "BOOM!"

Julie Boboolie, the head of the Amicable Representatives of Kismet, entered, and the air seemed to suck itself out of the room. As it does when a boss takes over. With her were John John Bobahn, a man in his thirties dressed like a construction worker, and an older, graying man, wearing a drab brown robe and sporting a Grateful Dead dancing bear tattoo on his right hand. When he made a fist, the dancing bear danced. And when the dancing bear danced, the older man giggled. He was giggling right now, because the dancing bear was dancing, because the older man was making a fist. Duh.

Julie took the seat at the head of the table. John placed a stack of papers and a calculator on the table and sat next to Linda. The older man sat at the other head of the table, about ten seats away, staring at his dancing bear fist. Julie pulled out a briefcase and placed in on the table and opened it. She pulled a piece of paper out of the briefcase and placed it on the table in front of her seat. "Gentlemen. Ladies."

"Hi Julie," Bill said.

"Been a long time," Linda said.

"Hi Julie," Sunflower said, and handed Julie a small sunflower.

"Thanks. I suppose you're all wondering why the Amicable Representatives of Kismet are meeting again," Julie said.

"No, we thought we were just here to watch you floss your teeth," Bill said. Last time they met Julie liked his jokes, so he thought he'd be the court jester again. He was already bored with this, so what the hell.

"Ha ha," Julie replied, and smiled. "Bill, it's been a long time, but you really haven't lost your – your – your whatever that is. Can everyone take a seat please?" She looked up and saw that everybody was already seated. "Good. First of all, I'd like to reintroduce the group, since some of you have not seen each other in damn near two thousand years. I mean, you'd think that a committee of this magnitude would meet more often, but – sorry, I'm not going to complain. This is Sunflower, Linda, John, Bill, and I think you all remember Noah." She pointed around the room to each person and finally to the older man at the other end of the table. Everybody looked at him with blank faces, like they were staring at a math problem they couldn't solve.

"Noah, of the Ark?" she asked, and raised her eyebrows. She looked around the table and saw no signs of recognition.

"You know," she said, and started singing, "Noah built the Arky, Arky." Still, blank expressions all around.

"Oh, come on!" she continued, and started singing again. "The Lord told Noah, to build him an Arky, Arky, The Lord told Noah, to build him an Arky, Arky, build it out of gopher barky, barky."

Bill smiled. Barky barky; NOW he remembered that song. Barky barky always made him laugh. And now he remembered that Noah guy. But he looked a bit older than the last time they met. Maybe 2,000 years ages a guy if he doesn't take care of himself.

Linda and Sunflower both smiled as well. The catchy song that went along with the old guy at the end of the table seemed to have fired up the neurons in their brains responsible for remembering stuff from 2,000 years ago.

"Good," Julie said. "Now - hey, does anybody know where Steve is?" She looked around the table; Linda, Sunflower and Bill all shook their heads, while Noah sat at the other end of the table and glared at everybody else, all at once. "No? Playing hooky while the rest of us work, apparently. All righty, then, down to business without them. Ladies and Gentlemen, we have a problem."

"A problem?" Linda asked.

"What kind of problem?" John asked.

"Are you going to spit it out or do we need to do the Heimlich on you?" Bill said, as he congratulated himself for his on-point jokes.

"Is that more of that – what do you call that? Humor? Is that more of that - humor, is it? - Bill?" Julie asked, her face as sarcastic as her words. She paused for a moment in the quiet room. "People, Chris wants to set sail again."

"On a three hour tour?" Bill said, and nobody smiled or made a noise. "You all suck. Nobody in this room thinks I'm funny."

"Whew," Linda said to Julie, "I thought you were going to say we're out of peanut butter and banana sandwiches. Wait – set sail? Is that why barky barky boy is here?" She pointed at Noah, at the other end of the table, glaring at the entire universe, all at once.

The others looked at Julie with muted anticipation, like they wanted to know the answer to the question but they didn't want Julie to know they wanted to know the answer to the question. Like they didn't want their curiosity to catch her attention, lest she pick them to do her evil set-sail bidding.

"That is exactly why he's here," Julie said.

"I heard that!" Noah replied, his voice a raspy muted roar that wouldn't be out of place in a Mel Brooks movie. "No, that's not why I'm here, so get it out of your pretty little heads. I am not setting sail again. My shrink says that the post-traumatic stress from the last little cruise has not yet cured, and I am not doing it again. Is that clear? Not doing it again."

He looked around and saw nothing but blank faces.

"Let me spell it out for you." He got up from his seat, approached the white board behind him, and started writing on it with an orange dry-erase pen. "N-O-T D-O-"

"Relax, Noah," Julie said, "Chris says you don't have to go again as long as you have a note from your psychiatrist. You do have a note, right?"

"Look at me, man!" Noah said, pointing at himself. "I'm a wreck! My hair is falling out, I look like I'm three thousand years old..."

"You *are* almost that old," Bill said under his breath.

"...I talk to my imaginary groupies, I'm a mess! I really need a note? I'm not going again! I can't take it! That's all there is to it! Note or no note!"

"You need a note," Julie said. Noah walked over the table next to the white board, pulled out some paper and a pen, and started writing as Julie continued. "Chris's never going to buy it without a note. Everybody wants you to go. You did so well last time. Why not go again? I mean, you take forty days, forty nights, you hang out on a cruise ship sipping exotic drinks with umbrellas in them, then the rain stops and you have the entire planet to yourself! Mostly! What could be better? It's like a forty day vacation! Hell, I'd do it, if I could. But, like the committee said, 'Miss Boboolie, you're not qualified,'" she said, with air quotes, her voice barely restrained from turning into a hiss. "I mean, I took the swimming lessons, the CPR classes, I learned the difference between a cheetah and a jaguar, I've watched 13 'Love Boat' marathons on television –"

Noah looked up from his paper at Julie and smiled like he was talking to a child. "You don't get it, do you? First of all, it's not just forty days and forty nights. That's just the rain. It takes seven months for the water to evaporate – and do you have any idea what seven months in a boat with geese and ducks and elephants smells like?"

"Ooh," Linda said, her face scrunched up like she had just eaten rancid meat.

"So you got a little wet and smelly," Bill said. "Quit whining and go."

Noah glared at Bill and walked towards Julie. "Look, Julie," Noah said, handing her a piece of paper, "here's my note. Can I go now?"

Julie took the note and started reading. "Post-traumatic stress blah blah blah can't be around animals for more than five minutes etcetera etcetera hates water, fear of people, hears voices – man, you've got it all – hey, it says here you have Arach - arach - arachibut - ibut - ibutyrophobia – arachibutyrophobia. Wow. What exactly is that?"

"It's the fear of peanut butter sticking to the roof of your mouth."

"Peanut butter?"

"There wasn't anything else to eat for the last 72 days of the voyage!"

"So these sandwiches here scare you?" Bill asked, pointing to the plate of sandwiches on the table.

"Anything made with peanut butter scares me, yes," Noah replied.

Bill picked up a sandwich and waved it at Noah. "Ooh, here's a big scary sandwich! Coming to get you!"

"Julie, can I go now?" Noah asked, nonplussed by Bill.

"Bill, you're not funny," Julie said. "And Noah, your note looks good. You may go, I guess."

Noah stuck his tongue out at everybody in the room, flipped them all off with both middle fingers, and gloriously shuffled out of the room, his brown robe dragging behind him like a misbehaving child forced to leave a movie theater, proud of the fact that his misbehavior got him kicked out of a movie theater.

"Can we get on with this? I have a 2:00 on the other side of the gates." Linda was clearly ready for this meeting to be over.

Julie took a sip from a water bottle labeled 'Soon To Be Wine, If You're Lucky,' and started. "The reason we are all meeting here today is because Chris wants to set sail again, and we are to organize the entire process. Obviously, we'll need a new person to go down there and get the animals and drive the boat this time, since Noah has Arana...arachibu... ...whatever, and I'm not qualified, because 'Love Boat Reruns are not instructional, Miss Boboolie.' I mean, c'mon! Who would have ever heard of the Lido Deck if not for 'The Love Boat?'" She took an audibly and overly deep breath as the others sat nervously, as one does when a leader has a public meltdown. "You don't, by any chance, have some issues, do you Julie?" Bill asked, while digging some of this morning's sausage out from between his right rear molars with another camouflage toothpick. He carried camouflaged toothpicks everywhere. They reminded him of his time on earth, when everything he had or wore was camouflage, even his underwear. Hey, you never know when you're going to get caught out in the forest with your pants off! "We all have issues, Bill," Julie replied. "All of us. It shouldn't get in the way of us fulfilling our dreams, though. Especially when our dreams are as simple as driving a stupid boat! All I ever wanted to do was to drive the flippin' boat!" She finished the bottle of water in her hand and threw it across the room, where it fell harmlessly to the floor as she put her head in her hands.

"Can we get on with this?" Linda asked.

"Okay, okay," Julie replied with a sigh as she lifted her head away from her hands, her hair mussed like she had just woken from a rough night's sleep. "You're right." She glared at life for a moment, looked down at the written agenda on the paper in front of her, and pointed at John, before saying, "At this time, I'd like to give the floor to John John Bobahn, the head of Ark construction."

"Hi, John," Sunflower said.

"Hi, John," Linda said, looking at her watch.

"John," Bill said without looking up. Last night's porterhouse didn't want to be removed from his left rear molar and was requiring all of his concentration.

"John, why don't you fill us in on your plans for the Ark," Julie said, as John ignored her and stared at Linda. "John? JOHN!"

"Yes, hot stuff?" John said, staring at Linda like she was a water cooler and he had been traveling through the dessert for seven weeks by himself. In the quiet conference room, the awkwardness was as heavy as an anvil. After a moment, John looked away from Linda and back to Julie. "Oh, right. Well, uh, I'll be heading down there tomorrow to sort of kick things off. We're going to need an environmental impact report, a building permit, a sizable bank account, a good set of engineered plans –"

"Why do you need all those things?" Bill asked.

"Well," John replied, "we're trying to make things as human as possible, so to speak. If we follow the rules and regulations of the earth society, we won't have humans rioting or, worse yet, trying to kill us. You know how they get. Plus I'm going to need to hire some human labor to help me build this thing. Unless, of course, you all are willing to come along and help out."

"No," everybody else said in unison.

"Which you obviously aren't," John continued. "So, without proper human permits and plans and currency, I won't be able to hire human labor. Which I'm obviously going to need."

"What's our time frame look like?" Julie asked.

John rifled through the papers in front of him on the table and settled on one. "I expect to have the boat ready for floating in about four months."

"Good," Julie replied, and spoke to everybody: "We have four months to collect all the animals and people for the Ark, and that leaves us –"

"People?" Sunflower interrupted. "You're taking people on the boat this time?

"There were people last time, Sunflower," Julie replied. "Don't you read your e-mails? There were eight people, to be exact. This time, Chris is insisting that we take two of each type of person on the boat so that society can rebuild quickly. I lobbied for four of each type of person, to cut down on the rebuild time lag, but -"

"That doesn't make any sense," Linda interrupted. "If Chris wants society to rebuild quickly, why destroy it in the first place? Humans are a cyclical breed. Give them enough time, they'll destroy themselves. They obviously don't need us to do it for them. If Chris wants to start the world over, just wait around for a few hundred years, and the humans will eliminate themselves, and Chris can have a clean slate to work with. And we can all go home. And two of each type of person? Like two architects? Two convenience store clerks? Two bank robbers? What's the point of two bank robbers?"

"Well, apparently," Julie said, "humans are basically good people. They've gotten a little off track and they need a warning shot, that's all. And, yes, two of each type of person -"

"A warning shot?" Bill interrupted. "You call flooding the earth with water a warning shot? Wow. I'd hate to see what happens if the they really screwed up."

"Now wait a minute," John said. "That's a lot of people. I didn't plan on that many people going on this boat. I'm going to have to rethink this. We're going to need a much bigger boat than I planned for, so it might be closer to -" He reached for the calculator, punched some keys, made a concerned face, and set the calculator down on the table. "Eight months."

"Eight months?" Julie asked. "Can you work double shifts or something? We really want this done in the next six months so that the new society can start soon. Get things back on track and all that. Besides, hurricane season is coming. And if Chris delays hurricane season, the earth people will wonder what's going on. We want no suspicion."

"Well," John replied, "I'll see what I can do, but I can't guarantee anything."

"Are we bringing any plants on this people-filled boat?" Sunflower asked.

"No," Julie replied. "Chris believes that the planet earth will regenerate its plant life once the water subsides, and with all the water the soil will have become saturated –"

"You can't bring humans with all their waste and their agendas and their meanness and bring animals with all their – their – their fur and not bring plants!" Sunflower interrupted, her young face as red as a canned beet. "That's discrimination. What did plants ever do to you?"

"Uh-oh," Bill said, looking up from extracting Tuesday night's pork chop from between his two front teeth, "looks like we got ourselves a nutcase."

"Look, Sunflower," Julie said, her face a mix of exasperation and retirement, "I realize that you are named after a plant and your parents were granola heads from Boulder, Colorado, and all that, but there's simply no room on any reasonable boat for every tree, every bush, and every type of grass. We would need a boat the size of the Exxon Valdez to pull that off. And that would definitely attract the wrong kind of earthly attention. So it's not going to happen."

"Well, then," Sunflower said, her eyes atwinkle, "what are the vegetarian people on the boat going to eat?"

"That's a damn good question," Linda said.

"Well, hell, that's simple," Bill said. "Just don't allow any of them tofu-eating fruitcakes on your boat. Then sit around and have a steak dinner every night. Hell, for that I'll drive your boat. As long as you bring three of every animal."

"Three?" John asked. "Why three?"

"So I can shoot one and you'll still have two animals left," Bill said. "A man has to get his target practice in. And have steak dinners!"

"You're a pig," Sunflower said.

"No, but I like to eat pig. Soo-wee!" Bill's pig impression filled the room, like a fart after a night full of bean burritos.

"Well," Sunflower said, ignoring Bill and turning back to Julie, "if you aren't bringing any plants on the boat, I'm attending this meeting under protest." She climbed up on top of the table, adjusted her sunflower sun dress, and sat down cross-legged atop the table. For a moment, Bill thought she was cute. For a moment. Then the elk in her dress reappeared and he wished he'd had his rifle. Again. "I'm calling this my Plant-In," she said, her lips pouty. "Or my Summer of Leaf. If it doesn't perform photosynthesis, I don't want to talk about it. I hope all those humans die from lack of fiber in their diets. Or mad cow disease. Or…hoof and mouth disease. Or, West Nile disease….H1N1…..you all suck."

Steve Easdale, fresh from his unevenly successful appearance at this week's Open Mic Monday, entered the room, clad in blue jeans, sneakers, and an Elvis '68 Comeback Special t-shirt. He was yet again a lamb in a room full of lions, a fact that was completely unknown to him.

"Hi everybody," Steve said, enthusiastically waving to everybody with his right hand. "Sorry I'm late. I was jamming with Prince and The King at Open Mic Monday, and time got away from me. Plus Elvis made some incredible peanut butter and banana sandwiches for lunch! Did I miss anything? I saw that Noah guy out in the hall – he mentioned a cruise? With animals? Said I'd enjoy it. I could use a vacation. Would it be like a safari cruise? That sounds like fun. What, do they put the animals on a boat so the passengers can get up close and personal? That'd be -"

"Well, Steve, hello," Julie interrupted. "We are just talking about that right now. Your vacation. We are talking about your vacation right now. Yes. Yes, indeed. Your vacation."

The rest of the room, except for Steve, slowly nodded in knowing agreement, as if they had actually been talking about Steve's vacation. He sat in the high-backed pleather-bound conference room chair at the head of the table that had been vacated by Noah.

"You know this was an all-hands meeting, right?" Julie said, glaring at Steve.

"I know," Steve said, "but the sandwiches -"

"So, Julie," Linda interrupted, "what kinds of animals should go on Steve's vacation?"

"I like the way you say that," John said, staring at Linda like a hungry man stares at a cooked lobster.

"Funny you should ask," Julie replied, "because we do need to discuss the animals on Steve's safari cruise. That's next on the agenda."

"Bring any animal you can shoot," Bill said, separating Wednesday night's dessert from his face. "And then eat it."

"What about lemmings?" Linda asked. "I mean, if you're really into suicide, I suppose. I kid," she said with a straight face. "But, really, assuming the flood waters subside from the planet earth and the ecosystems of said planet reestablish themselves, the Arctic climates of the planet will require lemmings. In a tundra environment, lemmings are the low mammals of the food chain, which means they are the main source of food necessary to sustain the food chain. Therefore, if you assume an Arctic climate will return to the planet earth, then yes, you need lemmings."

Julie pulled her glasses down from her eyes for a moment and looked at Linda. "Damn, you're smart."

"Hey, wait a minute -" Steve said, and stood up, his pale hands flat on the bland white melamine conference table in the bland white conference room in Heaven D.

"I think that instead of analyzing every animal known to

the planet earth – which might take several thousand years, and I don't have time for that – it would be in our best interests to take a good clear overview of which animals we aren't taking," Linda continued, ignoring Steve. "For instance, there are over 100 subspecies of the common house fly. We don't want to bring all of them, do we?"

"I thought," Steve said, "that this was going to be a cruise -"

"No, we don't," Linda continued, answering her own question. "Let's just bring two house flies and over time, they'll adapt to their surroundings and evolve into 100 new subspecies. It's that simple. Start with the basics and let them evolve again. Assuming everything stays the same down there and the planet is still fit for life – the last time I checked the ozone was still intact, barely – the evolution should be nearly the same as last time."

"What about useless animals, like, say, the West Highland Terrier?" Bill asked, looking up from the pile of used camouflaged toothpicks on the table in front of him. They really weren't camouflaged against the white melamine table top, because he could still see them, but boy if he were out in the forest…nobody would even know he had toothpicks. He smiled at the concept of unknown toothpicks.

"What about really ugly animals, like the platypus?" Sunflower asked from her place atop the table. "That thing looks like it was made from spare parts."

"What about sloths?" Bill asked. "They set a pretty bad example for the rest of the animal kingdom. And snails? If you leave snails behind, you'll piss off the French! Even more than they already are pissed off!"

"Oh, brother," Linda said.

"What about leeches?" Sunflower asked.

"They suck. Huh-huh," Bill said, as the room stayed silent. "And you all suck, 'cuz that was a good one. Wait, wait - what about Shih-tzus? The only cool thing about them is their name."

"You guys think this is funny, don't you?" Julie asked.

"Well, isn't it?" Bill asked. "I mean, the whole idea that we're going to build a big huge boat and stuff it full of animals and people is –"

"And no plants," Sunflower interrupted, and folded her arms together like a petulant child.

"And no plants, right, the whole idea is rather ridiculous," Bill said. "It's like a bad Hollywood movie."

Steve loudly spoke from his standing position at the head of the table. "Oh, I know what's going on here. This is no vacation cruise, is it? This is some sort of mission, isn't it? For me! Well, I'm not doing your dirty work for you, no way." He folded his arms and made his best pouty face. At least that's what his mom called it growing up. And more than once his best pouty face had gotten him out of a jam with his mom. Yeah, he might have been the only kid in the history of the world to have that tactic actually work on a parent.

"Steve, how many work committee meetings have you been to this year?" Julie asked.

"Well," Steve began, his young face one of conviction, "I went to the – no, I missed that one because Janis Joplin was singing in the town square. Okay, well, I went to the – no, I overslept that one. Um, wow, so I guess you could say I've been to, well, none of the work committee meetings this year." He smiled a smile that said, 'that's not bad, right? Oh please let it not be bad.'

"And Steve," Julie asked, "how much work have you done this year while everybody else at this table has been working forty hour weeks?"

"That's a good question," Bill said, staring at Steve, his Elvis '68 Comeback Special t-shirt askew as if it were trying to escape.

"Forty hour weeks?" Linda said. "Speak for yourself. More like eighty."

"What is this?" Steve asked, his voice rising in desperation.

"Group, I propose that Steve drives the boat," Julie said. "All in favor?" "Aye!" everybody in the room except Steve said, grins on their faces like they had just hit a jackpot in Vegas.

"Opposed?" Julie asked.

"AYE!" Steve yelled.

Julie pulled out her cell phone and pushed one button with her finger.

"I'm not driving your boat!" Steve yelled. "I don't know anything about humans! I can barely speak their language! Besides, I've got things to do up here! The King wants to sing Peace In The Valley again on Sunday at church in a duet with Billie Holiday!"

Julie spoke into her phone. "Hello, Chris? Yeah, Steve Easdale is going to drive the boat. Since I'm not 'qualified.' Yeah. He volunteered."

"NO I DIDN'T!" Steve yelled.

"Yes, I think we're ready to begin," Julie said into her phone. "Very good. Thank you. Good bye."

"What have you done?" Steve asked in sheer desperation. It was a question he would soon know the answer to, as lambs often do when confronted with lions. Unfortunately.

INTERLUDE 1

Donna Wedbetter had been a newscaster for ten years and, as such, was nearing the end of her career. Not yet, really, but she could feel it. The TV station she worked at, KDOG San Diego, had taken to hiring younger, more attractive female reporters who weren't afraid so show some skin and young, hunky male hipster reporters who looked like lumberjacks. Donna had heard that KDOG's numbers were down, so she guessed they were trying to appeal to a younger, hipper demographic, and she knew that that process would eventually lead to her demise. She wasn't unattractive by any means and she was very good at her job, but she was in her thirties. And she knew that in the shallow world of TV journalism, her 'best used by' date was, yes, in her thirties.

"Are we going to need an umbrella or a parka? That's the question our city asks tonight." Donna put on her best comfy smile - that's what her bosses called it, her 'comfy smile,' because it made people comfortable with her - and started reading the news from the TelePrompTer in front of her. "Good evening, and welcome to

the late edition of the early news. I'm Donna Wedbetter, and in tonight's top story, strange weather patterns seem to be gripping our city. West of us we can see clouds in the shapes of - well, they're cloud shaped, and east of us we've received reports of watermelon-sized ice-balls. Watermelon? What the -" She turned to the techies in the wings and asked, "can that be right?" One techie nodded his head. "It is right? Okay." Donna turned back to face the camera and continued. "Ace reporter Derek Deckenblacker is east of us right now and brings us this live report. Derek?"

On the screen in front of her a lumberjack with a microphone appeared. Or, really, it was that dumbass Derek Deckenblacker. He was a sweet kid, Donna thought, but oh so dumb. Like maybe he had gone to lumberjack school, where all they taught was lumber and jacking; they didn't teach logic and common sense. Because sadly, he was very much lacking in both. Still, he must have had the 'look' the station was looking for, because here he was, all beard and brawn and goofy grin and dumb brain. If he was Donna's little brother she would have beaten the crap out of him.

"Yes, Donna?" Derek's visage filled the screen for Donna and the viewers at home. And then a moment of awkward silence.

"Uh, you're experiencing ice-balls, right, Derek?"

"You wanna tell us about it, Derek?"

Derek's eyes widened like life had just hit his system. "Oh, right, right. Donna, we are experiencing ice-balls the likes of which haven't been seen since my Aunt Mable used to throw giant ice-balls at us in the field near her house back in Iowa. Ah, yes, Aunt Mable. She would always try to pass off her ice-balls as Snow Cones, and then when my brother and I would try to catch them with our mouths, we'd always end up in the hospital."

"She sounds pretty sadistic," Donna said, thinking that if Derek were Donna's little brother she would have put him in the hospital more than once. Via ice-balls, rocks to the head, titty twisters, wet willies, or hertz donuts. Or hell, all of the above. At the same time. Donna was a vicious big sister. And Derek was a dumb little brother.

"Indeed."

"Derek?"

"Yes?"

"Is there a story you want to tell us?"

"I just did."

Donna turned to the techies in the wings again. "Can you get me some competent reporters?" Then she put back on her comfy smile and turned to the cameras. "In other news…"

SCENE 2

Present Day. Thursday.

J im Johnson waited for his wife Ann to finish putting on her
face, or whatever she did to make herself pretty or whatever.
Jim didn't give a crap; dinner reservations were at 7:00 at
Chez Cul, with one of Jim's biggest clients. That's what he really
cared about. Westerberg Mars Stinson and Stinson, Jim's law firm,
were poised for a major breakthrough, and tonight's dinner with
Bob Dunlap, the head of product development at a major world-
wide security provider, would help expedite that breakthrough
dramatically. And perhaps help Jim finally make partner. That's
what Jim Johnson cared about. Making partner. Not what his wife
did to make herself up.

"Almost ready, honey?" he called to the bedroom of their 50th
floor condo in Trump Tower overlooking San Diego Bay.

"Do you think it's going to rain?"

Without rotating his head, Jim rolled his eyes to the sliding

glass door off the kitchen. The sky outside was dark and angry, like a father who had just discovered his son was stealing candy bars from Safeway. Yep, looked like rain. In San Diego. Where it never rains. Weird.

"Looks like rain, honey." He sighed. Waiting for his wife was not one of his favorite past times. He wouldn't even bring her, honestly, except Bob Dunlap was bringing his own wife, and Jim had found, from experience, that two couples close a deal much better than one couple and a third wheel.

"Will you grab my coat out of the closet?"

Damn, Jim thought. Do I have to do everything?

The doorbell chimed, and once again Jim remembered how much he hated the theme from 'Titanic,' the movie. Yes, that was the doorbell tone that Ann picked out. She and her fucking interior designer did that one day when he was at work. Once again Jim remembered how much he hated interior designers, too.

"Can you get that?" Ann asked from the bedroom.

Get the coat, get the door, Jim thought to himself. How many arms do you think I have? Ann was a pain in the ass, but Jim had found, from experience, that married attorneys at Westerberg Mars Stinson and Stinson did much better than single attorneys, so he kept her around. And, he thought, he kinda liked her. Sometimes.

He went to the front door, which was clad completely in brushed aluminum. It matched the windows and sliding glass door, but not the doorbell chime. 'Titanic?' Really? He wanted to fire Ann's fucking interior designer, but she insisted that Sergio understood her and *got* her, so much so that they had started going to yoga together. Which, to Jim, was perfectly fine. The less time he had to spend with Ann the more he kinda liked her. Sometimes.

He looked through the brushed aluminum peephole and saw a kid. Well, he was younger than Jim, anyway, by several years.

Maybe even fifteen or twenty years younger. Light brown hair, carrying a notepad, dressed like a salesman. Fuck.

He opened the door and, knowing that the kid salesman would launch into some spiel, immediately started talking.

"Look, buddy," he began. "We bought the special vacuum you guys sell, we already take the newspaper – for some godforsaken reason - and my wife doesn't need any more magazines. Why don't you call on Unit Forty Six? I hear they're in the market for another year of *The Weekly World News.*"

"But -" the kid salesman replied, and Jim slammed the door in his face.

"Who was it?" Ann was obviously still getting ready, as her voice barreled in from the bedroom. Jim checked his watch; they would need to leave soon to make that Chez Cul reservation. Women. Yeesh.

"Nobody, dear," Jim lied. "If I told you it was a salesman, we'd own a new box of seventy five bags of microwave popcorn inside of five minutes," he muttered to himself, low enough that Ann wouldn't be able to hear. If she knew he was making fun of her, she'd probably move even slower and they'd be late to their dinner with Bob Dunlap. And that wouldn't look good. Jim knew that from experience as well.

The theme from 'Titanic' played on their doorbell chime again. Fuck.

"I'll get it again," Jim yelled towards the bedroom. "Are you almost ready?" He looked through the peephole and saw the same kid standing there. They must be taught by their sales leaders to be persistent, Jim thought. He sold candy bars, magazines, and candles when he was in Boy Scouts as a kid; he remembered what a pain in the ass it was. And how many times he had a door slammed in his face.

So he opened it again.

"Is this the Johnson residence?" the kid asked, his face a meld of wonder, determination, and resignation. Like a salesman, Jim thought. Just like a salesman. And he knew that this was the Johnson residence, so this salesman must have a list of all the people who live in this building, which would be odd. The HOA swore up and down that no ownership list has ever gone out to anyone. There was no privacy anymore.

"Look, buddy," Jim started. He felt for the kid, but at the same time he knew who was behind the kid: some 'charitable' organization that used 97% of its donations for 'expenses' and 3% for actual charity. Yeah, it was bullcrap. "I give to the United Way at work, and I support the homeless down on the corner with my uneaten portions of Big Macs, and I really do care about orphans in third world countries. Really." Jim opened his wallet and handed the kid a dollar bill. A souvenir, really, of the connection that Jim was sure he and the kid had made. "Here's a dollar bill, go buy yourself a cup of coffee."

The kid stood there, a dollar bill in his free hand, looking for all the world like somebody who expected more from life. Much more. Jim sighed and decided to help the kid out.

"Here, kid, here's another dollar – take the two and buy yourself a short latte."

"A what?" Clearly the kid didn't drink coffee. Shit, Jim thought. And then he shut the door on the kid's face. If the generation gap between Jim and the kid salesman was such that they couldn't even relate on a coffee level, there was no reason to continue the relationship, Jim thought.

"Fucking salesman," Jim said out loud, as Ann entered the room. She was a striking woman; beautiful pale skin, a little black dress that was as universal as television remote controls, and black hair styled into a bob, to go with black heels on her feet. She really was a striking woman; too bad she was also a complete pain in the ass.

"And who was that, my dear?" she asked, her bob bobbing

around like it was in a heavyweight fight.

"It was nobody, really," Jim replied.

"Well, you sure had a long conversation with nobody," she replied, her white skin glowing under the LED lights of their condominium. "Nobody wouldn't happen to be selling candy for a school fundraiser, would they? I know how you feel about 'kids selling crap,' but if they're selling it for a school fundraiser, count me in!"

"It was nobody, really," Jim repeated, his voice monotone to convey unimportance. It was a technique he learned at law school, alongside other such valuable techniques as how to hide your booze in leather bound books, how to baffle everybody with bullshit, and how to be a big enough of an asshole to make partner at Westerberg Mars Stinson and Stinson. Truly, law school played a huge role in Jim's life.

"Uh huh," Ann said, brushing by Jim as the theme from 'Titanic' played again. "I'll get this one."

She opened the door and, yes, the kid was still there. Jim hoped there would be a survey at the end of this financial transaction – because now that his wife was involved, there would *definitely* be a financial transaction, that much he knew - where he could give the kid high marks for perseverance, which was another technique taught at law school. In fact, Jim thought, the kid would make a good lawyer. Speaking of lawyers, Jim thought, we need to get going. He went to get his coat from the coat closet.

"Now listen here -" the kid started, and then he saw Ann. She was not the one who had slammed the door in his face twice, and his face softened. "Oh, hello, ma'am. Are you Ann Johnson?"

Ann's eyes lit up and she stood a little taller, like a sophomore being noticed by the starting quarterback. "How did you -" she stammered, as her mouth lifted into a semi-smile - "know my name?"

"I've come for your -" the kid started again, and then looked through his notepad, like he was digging through a newly opened box of cereal, looking for the toy inside. "Uh, cat," he said, and looked up. "Right. Cat. I've come for your cat."

"My cat?" Ann asked, her face as quizzical as the night was young.

"Don't buy anything," Jim yelled from the coat closet. He knew that it was a futile attempt to sway her mindset, because of course she was going to buy whatever the kid was selling, but he was a lawyer and could never resist attempts to sway mindsets. Futilely or otherwise.

"My cat?" Ann repeated.

The kid looked down at the huge pile of paper on his clipboard, which Ann now noticed was a checklist of some sort.

"Yes, that's what it says," the kid said, pointing at the paper with his finger. "Cat."

For just the right amount of an awkward amount of time, Ann and the kid stood face to face at her brushed aluminum door in her fiftieth floor condo overlooking San Diego Bay, their eyes locked, the quiet sound of the pitter-patter of the beginning of a rain storm the only sound.

"Miss Johnson, it's very important. Is your cat here?"

Jim reappeared with his coat, Ann's coat, a couple of umbrellas, and his car keys. In his hand, so the kid could see them. Jangling, so his wife could hear them. Again, trying to sway mindsets, both of the kid and his wife, because if he couldn't get them both to realize that Chez Cul wouldn't hold their reservation for more than five minutes past the reservation time – it was a *very* popular place - then they'd be late and Jim would lose Bob Dunlap and neither he nor Ann would be able to afford a new vacuum cleaner or magazines or whatever the kid was selling. Or buying. Something about a cat?

"What do you want with my cat?" Ann started, and Jim knew he was too late to sway her mindset. Once she started... "You're not going to try and make me get Donald J Trump neutered again, are you?"

The kid chuckled. "You named your cat Donald J Trump? Oh, that's too good."

Ann continued on, undeterred by the interruption. "I told you people last time – Donald J is a purebred something or another, and until we find out what that something or another is and how much his babies might be worth on the Home Shopping Spree, he's keeping his Johnson attached to his body. So to speak."

Jim sighed. It was true. He wanted to neuter Donald J Trump way back when, but every time he tried to find the cat he was nowhere to be found and eventually Jim gave up on the idea. Despite the occasional random spraying around the condominium. That's why they had house cleaners come to the condominium every Friday. Jim worked long hours all week but took weekends off, and when Saturday rolled around he was happier when the condominium was clean. And Donald J Trump's random spraying was gone.

"Is your cat here?" the kid asked. "It's starting to rain."

"You still haven't told me what you want with him," Ann said, her face skeptical, like a mom being told by her chocolate-faced son that no, he didn't eat all the chocolate candy bars.

Jim jangled his keys to no effect and decided to be more direct about this. "Short latte not enough for you, huh, buddy? How about I give you enough for a tall latte? Grande? Vente? Mocha? Machiatto? Frapuccino? Will you leave us alone for a Frapuccino?" He pulled his wallet out; it was the natural evolution of mindset swaying, the next step after key jangling.

"I don't know what those things are," the kid replied, "but I need your cat."

"Donald J been out cavorting again, has he?" Jim asked. "He's a lady killer. A real tiger, you know? Grabs 'em all by the pussy, even." He slapped the kid on the shoulder with his free hand.

Buddying up to the kid was the next step of mindset swaying after offering the kid money. Sometimes, Jim learned at law school, when you became somebody's friend, the path to them agreeing with your position cleared up dramatically. Fake friendship was like a machete that way.

"Look, is your cat here?" Dammit, Jim thought, he went too far. The kid was exasperated now. Shit. Going too far was Jim's weakness, as his partners at Westerberg Mars Stinson and Stinson would attest to. Sometimes an idea implanted itself in his brain and simply took over.

Fuck the exasperated kid, Jim thought, he had reservations with Bob Dunlap at Chez Cul. It was time to end this.

"What the hell do you want with our cat?" Jim asked, stone faced and direct.

"I need to take him with me," the kid replied, as the sound of rain on the windows of the condominium picked up. "It's starting to rain, so I'm prepared to offer you -" He looked down at his clipboard. "Five thousand dollars for your cat."

Jim and Ann looked at each other quizzically and back at the kid, also quizzically. None of this made sense.

"No," Ann said.

"No," Jim said, and Ann smiled at him. Sometimes, he thought, her husband wasn't such a lawyer asshole. And then he discarded that thought and centered himself back to lawyer asshole. "Make it twenty thousand and you have a deal." Five thousand dollars was a good offer, but he was a lawyer and he knew that if the kid really wanted his cat, five thousand wasn't the real number. The first offer was *never* the real number. And twenty thousand dollars was probably not the real number either, but he was a lawyer and had learned that a counteroffer was never the real number, either. Shoot for the moon, take the earth.

"Jim!" Ann stared at her husband, who knew what she was thinking. What the hell was wrong with him? Sell Donald J

Trump? They had never had any kids, because Jim was always too focused on his work to even try to be a father, so their cat was their family. And twenty thousand dollars could not replace family. *That's* what she was thinking.

"Okay," the kid replied. "You humans always want more, don't you? So gluteus."

"What?" Ann asked, her face incredulous, like she couldn't believe her chocolate faced son ate a seventeenth chocolate candy bar.

"I think the word you're looking for is 'gluttonous,'" Jim replied, warmly, "and yes, we always do want more. Please, come in. What was your name?" He stepped aside and waved the kid in.

"Oh, thank you. I'm Steve. Steve Easdale."

"Any relation to that John Easdale guy on TV?" Ann asked. Jim had no fucking idea who she was talking about, but at the same time he didn't care. She watched TV constantly and he, frankly, didn't. He watched one of her favorite cooking shows for about five minutes once and fell asleep and that was that.

"We're all related in one way or another, Miss," Steve said, looking down at his checklist.

"Yes, that's true, isn't it?" Ann replied.

"Have a seat, Mister Easdale," Jim replied to her reply. "Can I get you anything to drink?" In his mind, all he was going to do was turn Donald J Trump over to this kid and get paid. And still have time to make his meeting at Chez Cul with Bob Dunlap, which means he would get paid a second time. Yes, he was that confident in his own abilities, because why the fuck not? He was Jim Johnson, and he LOVED getting paid twice in one day. He loved it so much he saw himself as a porn star in the law business; a porn star who could get it up more than once in one day. Twice, even. Steve sat down in the Eames Chair in the front foyer of Jim and Ann's condo. Normally, somebody besides himself sitting in the Eames Chair would bother the fuck out of Jim, but tonight he kept his eyes on the prize. The twenty thousand dollar prize.

"Something to drink?" Jim repeated.

"No, thanks," Steve replied. "Can you get your cat? I'm in a hurry."

Jim thought about this request; it was reasonable, he supposed. Except for one small detail. A detail that he, as an almost-partner at Westerberg Mars Stinson and Stinson, understood completely.

"Show us the money." Jim, it should be noted, was also a big fan of the 1996 Tom Cruise vehicle, 'Jerry Maguire.'

"Jim, don't be rude!" Ah, cute pain in the ass Ann...also known as Miss Fucking Manners. At least in Jim's head.

Steve took a deep breath. "You just don't stop, do you?" He reached into the back pants pocket of his salesman pants, pulled out his black leather wallet, and opened it. "Oh, shill, I only have fifty dollars."

"Do you mean shit?" Jim asked. Ann glared at him like he was offering to bang her sister. She had no perspective. Salesmen don't care about manners.

"I must have spent all my money on the other animals. Dank."

"Damn?"

"I'll give you fifty bucks for your cat."

Jim chuckled. "Twenty thousand dollars is a much higher number than fifty bucks. You know that, right?" He glared at Steve with his eyebrows raised. This kid was a terrible salesman, as it turns out.

The Titanic theme played. Fuck, Jim thought. Another stupid salesman? He ignored Ann glaring at him and opened the door.

A butler stood there.

Yes, a butler.

An older man, not much hair on his head, but what there was was white. Black pants, black vest, black bowtie, white shirt, white gloves, white hair.

Holding a silver tray with cocktails balanced upon it.

"Your drinks, sir."

Jim paused for a moment. He didn't remember ordering any drinks. And the last time he forgot he ordered drinks was his last trip to Las Vegas, eight years ago. He hated forgetting that he ordered drinks so much he never went back to Vegas. Fuck that place. Fuck any place that made him forget he ordered drinks. Fuck any place that made Jim feel a loss of control.

He looked at Steve and Ann; both of their eyes were vacant. Who the fuck ordered drinks from a proper butler? When was the last time anybody actually had a proper butler? Not even the partners at Westerberg Mars Stinson and Stinson had proper butlers. Sure, they had mistresses who posed as maids and mistresses who posed as secretaries and mistresses who posed as nannies, but nobody had a proper butler. That would be uncouth!

"I didn't order any drinks," he replied, his eyes on the old man, whoever he was.

"Pleased to meet you," the butler replied, his eyes twinkling, his voice deep and seductive, like bourbon on a Friday afternoon. "Noah needs a beverage."

"Who's Noah," Jim asked. "What the hell are you talking about?" Jim quickly scanned the contact list embedded in his brain. Noah? Did he know anybody named Noah? It was an unusual name, and the closest Jim could come up with was 'Norah,' who was Jim's favorite waitress at his favorite lunch spot next to Westerberg Mars Stinson and Stinson's offices in Little Italy.

Norah was also Jim's lover.

His Tuesday lover.

She asked to be his Thursday lover, also, but Sherry had that covered.

Oh, yes, did she have that covered. She had it so covered that sometimes Sherry ended up being Jim's Friday lover as well. He figured it was all part of the path to making partner at Westerberg

Mars Stinson and Stinson. All the current partners had mistresses, and Jim had made it this far by gleaning behavioral examples from the people higher up on the corporate ladder than himself; mistresses was just the next step on that ladder.

"Your drink, sir," the butler said, and handed Jim a highball glass filled with a brown liquid. He smelled it; an old-fashioned. A very good old-fashioned. Whoever had sent this butler guy knew Jim very well, as a very good old-fashioned was his favorite drink.

He looked at Ann, who already had a glass of Chardonnay – HER favorite - in her hand and at Steve, who already had a mimosa in his hand.

Somebody was fucking with him.

The butler turned and left through the brushed aluminum front door.

"I don't usually drink on the job," Steve said, as Jim wondered if he was old enough to drink at all. "But since this is the last cat, why the hell not?"

"Who was that guy," Ann asked, as she sipped her wine. "Because this Chardonnay is *excellent.*"

"I don't know," Steve replied, "But these really are good drinks, aren't they?"

"Why did he call you Noah," Jim asked. It was almost time to go to Chez Cul, but he enjoyed solving mysteries – it's what led him to law, he always told himself - and this was turning into a weird mystery. And, really, not only did he enjoy solving mysteries, he *had* to solve mysteries. It's what made him a good lawyer. And, ultimately, what would make him completely miss his meeting at Chez Cul. "And why is ours the *last* cat?"

Steve took a gulp, paused, and looked at Jim. It was a look Jim recognized. It was a look of evasion.

"I can't tell you that," Steve said. Of course. Evasion. Hm-mmmmm. Something else was going on here, Jim thought Something weird. Something sci-fi weird, like the paperback novels Jim read when he was a kid. A mystery. A sci-fi weird mystery.

"Did our cat swallow some top secret microchip that contains the key to the future of the planet?" Jim asked. "Or something?" Sure, it was weird, and not really a theory he'd float in a courtroom, but this situation seemed like something he wouldn't run into in a courtroom. Somehow.

"Yeah, okay," Steve replied, between sips of his mimosa. "Something like that."

"Are we in the Twilight Zone?" Ann asked. "Yeah, is Rod Serling standing outside?" Jim asked. "That would make a lot of sense." He dialed up his Rod Serling impression; not only did he like paperback sci-fi novels when he was a kid, he was a huge Twilight Zone/Rod Serling fan. "This man, Steve, and this wealthy downtown couple and their cat, about to embark on a journey that could only take place...in the Twilight Zone."

"That's pretty good, man," Steve replied with a nod of his head. "I know Rod personally, and he'd be impressed with -"

"Rod Serling is dead." Jim took a sip of his old fashioned; it was as good as this situation was weird.

"Yeah, and you'll be dead soon, too," Steve replied, his eyes wide and his head nodding, as if though stating the inevitable. Jim wondered what the fuck was wrong with this kid. This kid knew Rod Serling, and he, Jim, was going to be dead soon? He recognized a legal smokescreen when he saw it, but this was a bit extreme if all the kid was trying to do was get his cat. He felt the mystery deepen in his mind, a bottomless canyon of whatthefuck.

"Dead?" Ann asked, her head tilted like a puppy who had just been told that her human was out of treats.

"Soon?" Jim asked, his eyes narrowed, his lips pursed, in a display of overall skepticism that rivaled that of the best mothers whose children had just told them that no, *they* didn't pee that wet bed and no, they didn't know who did.

"Shit," Steve replied. "No, no, that's not what I said. I said, uh -"

"OH MY GOD," Ann screamed right into Jim's ear as her drink glass crashed to the floor. "I KNOW WHO YOU ARE!"

Jim turned his head; his ears were going to ring for several minutes. He knew this because in 97% of the instances when Ann had epiphanies, she screamed them right into Jim's ear. Right or left, it didn't matter, both rang equally for several minutes afterwards. Normally he would have had earplugs in each ear because he was at home, but he was sure until now that they were going to go out tonight with other humans and he actually wanted to be able to hear those other humans. Not including his wife.

"YOU KNOW WHO HE IS?" Jim yelled, overcompensating for the lack of volume in his own ears. Normally he wouldn't have said anything at this moment and let his ears rest, but his desire to solve this weird mystery overrode every other instinct in his body.

"That guy – the guy with the drinks - called you Noah. You're Noah!" Ann turned and glared at Jim's face. "He's Noah FROM NOAH'S ARK!"

Jim had read every sci-fi book he could his hands on when he was a kid; Harlan Ellison, Phillip K. Dick, Bradbury, Wells, Heinlein. But he had never, in his lifetime, heard such a far-fetched plot for any story as the return of Noah. He shook his head, took one last drink from his old fashioned, and prepared to go to Chez Cul. He hoped he wasn't too late; he couldn't believe he spent so much time on this stupid kid and his stupid wife. He shook his head.

"You're kidding, right, Ann?"

"You're Noah from Noah's Ark," Ann exclaimed, finger pointed at Steve's chest. "And you're in our living room! Can I get your autograph?"

Jim rolled his eyes and wondered how much longer he could live with this crazy woman. He knew it dovetailed with the length of time he had to make partner at Westerberg Mars Stinson and Stinson, but right now he wasn't even sure he could wait that long. Noah? From Noah's Ark? What the fuck? "Jesus," he said, exasperated.

"Yes, honey," Ann replied. "That's his boss!"

"Dear," Jim said, his eyes firmly locked on Steve, who was staring at the ceiling like a child waiting for his parents to finish with parent-teacher conferences, "I hate to be the one to break it to you, but Noah from Noah's Ark has been dead for God-knows-how-long."

"Yes He does, honey. He does know how long."

"Ann!" Jim finally looked at his wife, who was looking at Steve like he was Bruce Springsteen or something. "Come on! This is obviously some sort of...just because this guy comes for our cat and there's a strange butler who calls him Noah and it's raining in San Diego where it never rains..." Jim stopped and listened. Yep, the rain was steady and steadily increasing. It was a sound foreign to his ears, really, because, well, San Diego.

"It IS raining," Ann replied, looking up at the ceiling. She turned her gaze to Steve. "Well, are you Noah? It would make sense. You want our cat, you're calling him the 'last cat,' you're freaking out about rain –"

"I wouldn't call it freaking out –"

Lightning struck the 50th floor of Trump Tower in San Diego bay and the lights went out. There, in the darkness, as the building shook around him, Jim had an epiphany. A deep, dark epiphany that fried his neurons, solved the mystery nagging at his brain, and changed his life.

"Holy shit," he muttered, "It really is you. It all makes sense."

"It really doesn't," Steve replied.

The lights came back on.

"Our cat is the last animal to go on the new Ark! Donald J Trump! Our stupid little horny cat!" Jim said.

"Take us with you," Ann said to Steve, who was licking his glass of mimosa.

"I can't."

"Why not?" she asked.

"Because," Steve sighed. It sounded like the weight of the world being lifted off of his shoulders. Or maybe onto his shoulders. It was hard to tell, but it was a heavy sigh. "Because your cat is the last animal to go on the freakin' boat. Every other animal on the list is accounted for."

"There's a list?" Ann asked.

"Well," Steve sighed again. Jim wondered if he was going to sigh every time he responded to a question. He knew a few judges who would throw the kid out of court for sighing that many times. "Yeah. How do you think we keep track of all this?"

"Put us on the list," Ann continued. Shit, Jim thought, that was a great idea. There was a list, he wanted to fucking be on it.

"You don't understand," Steve said, without sighing this time. "I don't make the list, I just enforce it. I'm just doing my freaking job. That's all I'm doing. My job. So I can go home."

"Who does make the list?" Ann continued.

"Who do you think?"

Who do we think, Jim asked himself. Who do we think? Who the fuck would make a list of animals to save while the rest of the planet drowned? God, that's who. Jim never was religious, really, but every time his parents dragged him to church on Sundays, he grew more skeptical. Why would a benevolent deity be so cruel to his creations? If God created us all, why the hell couldn't he fix us all without resorting to such drastic solutions as flooding the fucking planet? It never made sense to Jim. It was like the time he went up against a lawyer in court whose client was accused of simple embezzlement and, at the last minute, the accused killed himself. It seemed like a drastic solution to a very simple problem, in Jim's mind. Sure, the client was probably going to go to jail, but he would get out at some point. Unless he was dead, of course. And, as it turns out, he was dead. Hey, his choice. Even though it made no sense.

"Can we see the list?" Jim asked.

"Where is your cat?" Steve asked, and the tension in the room was as thick as a fancy cheese from the cheese shop downstairs. Ann would go down there and order a hunk of cheese and spend $45 or more and Jim always wondered why they didn't just buy Velveeta. Yes, he was that sophisticated. But hey, Velveeta was yummy. He even kept a slab of it in his desk drawer at the office. For snacking.

"The list," Jim repeated.

"The cat," Steve repeated, and the tension grew as thick as a slab of Velveeta cheese.

Jim knew how to defuse this. He was a lawyer, after all, and had learned defusion techniques from his seven years in law school and from his twelve years at Westerberg Mars Stinson and Stinson. So he reached into the cabinet next to Steve in the condo entry where they were all standing and pulled out his handgun. And pointed it at Steve's head. It might have been a bit drastic, sure, but Jim was certain, after the lightning epiphany, that this was a very important event in his lifetime. And he also knew from the epiphany that he had a calling. A calling from the Lord - or whoever - above. A calling to survive whatever was coming next so that he could practice law in the post-Ark world. Another thing he learned from his twelve years at Westerberg Mars Stinson and Stinson was that people needed him, and he was certain now that they would need him again after whatever happened next. Probably even more so than before whatever happened next.

Or so that's what was he was telling himself. It sure sounded better than "I just wanna not die," and everybody knows that lawyers are experts at rephrasing words so they sound better than they would coming from a non-lawyer.

"Let us see the list. Now."

Steve looked up to the condo ceiling like he was talking to God – or whoever. Jim recognized this look, too. Defendants in cases did it just before they broke.

"I don't recall this being part of the deal," he said to the ceiling. Or to God. *Was this really happening,* Jim asked himself as he pointed his gun at the head of a guy named Steve, who was really Noah. And Donald J Trump was going to be the last animal on the new Ark. Jim rubbed his temple with his free hand as he contemplated this turn of events. Surely this was the weirdest Thursday night of his life.

"Jim, put that thing away," Ann yelled at him. "Do you want to piss off the man – or woman - who makes the list?"

"LET US SEE THE LIST," Jim replied, not to Ann, but to Steve. If there was a fucking list, he wanted to see it and get this night moving. He had a gut feeling the list would affect the rest of his life.

Steve sighed an exasperated sigh. Yep, Jim thought, just like court. The defendant bitches to God about his circumstances, then he sighs, then he caves.

"You wanna see the list?" Steve asked, his face a frantic collage of sweat, concern, and outright indignation.

Jim cocked the gun that he was holding against Steve's head. He knew when it was time to apply pressure, and now was the time to apply pressure.

"Show us the list or I'll kill you," he said firmly to Steve. This was textbook 'win the case' bullshit that he was pulling here, but damn if it wasn't working. It always worked.

"Okay, OKAY." Yep, it always worked. Steve pulled out some papers from his clipboard and handed them to Jim. Holy shit, he thought, there's actually a list. This was real? He'd seen a lot of crazy shit in his law career, but never did he think he would see crazy Twilight Zone shit like the return of Noah. He trembled a little bit while he handed the list to Ann and kept his gun pointed at Steve's temple.

"Read the list," he said to Ann. "What's on it?"

"Well," she replied, her face as excited as a toddler's on Christmas morning. She put on her reading glasses and perused the list. "Let's see...I see two lions, two tigers, two bears, two mosquitoes..."

"Mosquitoes?" Jim asked.

"Yes, but the box is checked which probably means that they're already on the boat."

"You're taking mosquitoes on the Ark?" Jim asked Steve over the barrel of the gun. "Didn't you learn last time?"

"Hey, I don't make the damn list, alright?" Steve replied calmly. "You got a beef with the list, you take it up with the proper Australians."

"It's authorities, dumbass," Jim replied. "And I want to take the mosquitoes' place on the Ark. That's what I want in exchange for Donald J Trump."

"Again, I don't make the list. Alright? I don't make the list. Do you understand? I don't make the list, and I can't change the list!"

"I guess I'm going to have to shoot you," Jim said, pushing the barrel of the gun harder against Steve's head.

"Wait, Jim! I found something!" Ann exclaimed from the pile of paper she had laid out on the dining room table of their fiftieth floor Trump Tower condo overlooking San Diego bay. For a moment, Jim thought, she looked like a lawyer. And he liked her again. For a moment. "Right here on page 74, it says 'Two Dentists, Two Magicians, Two Married People –'"

"We're married," Jim replied, right into Steve's face, as if though he were cross examining Steve about his activities the night of the murder or something.

"Oh," Ann said, "but it looks like the Swansons next door were selected for that category."

Steve yawned and smirked at Jim, who was still pointing a gun at his head.

"THE SWANSONS?" Jim asked. He hated the Swansons. "Why the fuck would you take them on the Ark? They cheat at bridge! They borrow things and never return them! They voted for Hillary!"

"They don't clean up after their dog," Ann said, still looking at the list in front of her.

"Yeah!" Jim said, as he again pushed the barrel of the gun against Steve's head. "THEY. DON'T. CLEAN. UP. AFTER. THEIR. DOG." It was time for 'Bad Cop' in this solitary game of 'Good Cop/Bad Cop,' if Jim was going to close this case anytime soon.

"WAIT," Ann yelled from her list. She looked up at Jim and smiled. "Here, on page 216, 'Attorney.' That's you, honey!"

Steve laughed. "You're an attorney? I tried to convince Chris that we didn't need any of you on the cruise, but albatross."

"You mean alas," Jim replied. "And don't you recognize me from my commercial?" Jim put the gun down on the hallway table, cleared his throat, and put on his best 'pitchman on TV' voice, which sounded like a cross between Christopher Walken and a homeless seal. "Hi, I'm attorney Jim Johnson, and I can help you! Just like I helped this guy:" Jim cleared his throat and put on his best 'lawyer client on TV' voice, which sounded like a cross between Larry The Cable Guy and a homeless seal. "'Hi, I'm Joe Shmoe, and Jim got me $2.5 million dollars after a doughnut fell on my shoe and hurt my big toe.' That was one of my best spots ever."

"People seemed to really respond to that one," Ann said, not looking up from the list.

"Noah," Jim said to Steve, as he prepared to rest his case. "I'm ready to take my place on the Ark." Yep, Jim thought, that should do it. He went through every phase of everything he knew and he always won when he did that. Even in donuts-falling-on-shoes cases. Sure, that was a stupid case, but Jim won. And got paid. And sometimes it was all about getting paid. Well, really, Jim thought, all the time it was about getting paid. Let's not be dishonest about that.

"I'm not Noah, okay?"

"Sure," Jim said, "Steve, Noah, Gilligan, Captain Stubing, whoever you are. I'm ready to take my place on the Ark."

"But, Jim," Ann said, looking up from the list and right into Jim's eyes. She looked like she wanted to cry. "Randy Damon and Barbara Stinglemeyer are the two Attorneys who are going on the Ark. It says so right here."

"Randy Damon?" Jim asked. Randy Damon was a slimebucket. "You're taking Randy Damon? That guy's a slimebucket! He went after a little old lady because her cane accidentally touched his client on his butt!"

"And donuts falling on shoes don't make you a slimebucket?" Steve asked.

"I'm surprised you know that word," Jim said.

"I've met some slimebuckets in my time."

"Look, Noah," Jim continued, as he picked up and raised his pistol again and placed the barrel against Steve's temple. "I'm ready to take my place on the Ark now. I'm ready. Sure you know what that word means, yes? Ready?"

"Mr. Johnson, can you put the gun down?" Steve said. "Mrs. Johnson, can you please give me the list? Just for the hell of it, I'll check the list to see if there's some room for you, OK? The King is waiting for me and I don't have time for this nonsense."

"And it's raining," Ann said, staring out the window at downtown San Diego. Jim looked out; yep, there was some weird moisture falling from the sky. And the sky was dark. He wondered if he had accidentally moved to Seattle. Today, nothing would surprise him.

"Yes," Steve said from behind the barrel of Jim's gun. "Gun, Mister Johnson? Down, so I can look at the list?"

"Alright," Jim replied, as he put the gun down on the table in the foyer and Steve took the list and starting flipping through its pages. And then Jim's lawyer's mind kicked in again.

"Hey, Steve," he said with a friendly voice. Jovial, even. He was again practicing the 'be a friend' technique of lawyering, where he pretended to be a defendant's friend to glean information. It was an actual class at law school. A class Jim aced. "Is there a double income, no kids category? DINKs is what we call them."

Steve nodded his head and thumbed through a couple of pages in the list. "Yes, but that's full."

"Is there a wealthy couple living in a luxurious condominium with a single pet category?"Ann asked. Jim paused; damn, his wife was smart. For such a pain in the ass.

"Yes, but that appears to be full as well," Steve replied. "Look, the only things I have left are....well, earlier today, I had a male artist drop out – he said he wanted to hang around to paint the end of the world. Artists." He rolled his eyes and shook his head.

"I'm an artist," Jim said. All he really knew was that he needed to be on that ship when it sailed out of San Diego Harbor. If he had to be an artist or a hippie or a vegetarian for a moment – three things he would never actually be in real life, because GROSS - then he would.

"Jim?" Ann looked at Jim like a child looks at a father who has just announced he's moving in with the child's aunt. "Yeah, look," Jim said, as he grabbed a pencil and a napkin off of the entry credenza and drew a smiley face on the napkin. "I drew this picture. I'm an artist."

"Jim!" Ann said.

"Look, Mister Johnson," Steve replied. "There are specific rules to follow. You have to have been –"

"Jim! What about me?" Ann asked. Yeah, what about her? Jim looked at her and felt nothing; nothing compared to the nagging compulsion that he had to be on that boat. "If you go as an artist, what about me? What do I go as?"

"Who cares? I just need to get on that boat."

"Oh my God! You'd actually go without me?" Ann walked over and embraced Jim from behind, but he just stood there. Because if push came to shove – and it felt like they had left push behind and that this *was* shove, right here - yes, he would go without her.

Shit, he didn't even like her. Didn't she know that by now? Stupid women.

"So, am I in?" he asked. "Or do I need to get my gun again?"

"You are not in," Steve replied. "'Artist' is a mindset and a passion, not an obvious once-in-a-lifetime pencil drawing on the back of a napkin. You drew a smegma face."

"A smiley face," Ann replied, her face buried in Jim's back.

"I have a mindset!" Jim exclaimed. "I have passion! Look!" He took the pencil and drew a stick figure on the napkin. Fuck, he wished he had paid attention in art class. Fuck, he never took art class. Fuck, why don't law schools offer art class? "I drew two pictures! That's passion!"

Steve shook his head.

Jim threw the tray of orange M & M's that lived on the entry table onto the floor. "I can starve for my art!"

"I don't believe this," Ann said, as she let go of Jim's back and collapsed on the hallway floor.

"Call whoever's in charge of this thing and tell them I'm an artist and I'm going on the boat" Jim said to Steve.

"You are not an artist," Steve said.

Jim found his gun and pointed it at Steve's head again. "CALL THEM NOW!"

"Mr. Johnson," Steve said, "there are rules and regulations and qualifications, and you don't qualify. Even if I tried to put you on the boat, you'd just slip and fall on your way over there and end up in the hospital. Unqualified people do not make it on the boat. Under any circumstances. You don't understand who and what we're dealing with here."

"How can I qualify?" Jim asked. There was always a way. He was a personal injury attorney, the slippery-est, slimiest, most optimistic type of person on the planet; there was always a way.

"How can *we* qualify?" Ann asked. Always butting in, that woman.

"The only way you can qualify is if you're on the list," Steve said, pointing at the list as if to say, '*This* is the holy grail, and you aren't in it, so nyah nyah nyah nyah.' At least that's how Jim saw it. Little prick.

There was always a way, Jim thought, and then he had an idea. An epiphany, he would call it, if he were a religious man. He wasn't; he just wanted to be on that boat. He figured that in forty days and forty nights on the boat there were going to be some conflicts and he figured that a lot of the people on the boat were going to have money, because, really, would they let poor people on that boat? No, they wouldn't. Even if poor people were selected to be on the boat somebody with money would buy them out before they even got close to the boat, right? And if everybody on the boat had money and there were conflicts, they would all need an attorney, right?

Right. The slippery-est attorney this side of Saul Goodman.

Jim Johnson, at your service. With a new firm where he WAS partner. Johnson and Johnson, he'd call it. Or Johnson, Wanker, Pud, Pecker and Weiner. A name that was transparent and described what he did perfectly.

"Can a person move up the list?" he asked.

Steve cocked his head like a puppy, rolled his eyes up, and replied. "I've heard that's possible."

Newly energized with this idea and fully aware of what he needed to do, Jim Johnson grabbed his coat and the keys to his Audi R8 and headed towards the brushed aluminum door of his 50th floor Trump Tower condo overlooking San Diego Bay.

"I'll see you on the boat, Mister Noah."

"It's Steve."

"Mister Noah Steve Noah whoever the fuck you are." And Jim walked out the front door towards the elevators, towards his new life defending the occupants of the New World from each other. And then another epiphany hit him: *Flood insurance!* Surely nobody had flood insurance, right? He wondered to himself if he could sue Jesus Christ himself when this was all over. Think of the headlines!

As he pushed the button to take the elevator down, he heard the theme from Titanic and then his wife's voice through the slowly closing condominium front door.

"Jim, what about me?"

INTERLUDE 2

"Messenger from God or evil incarnate? That's the question our city asks tonight. Good evening, and welcome to the early edition of the late news. I'm Donna Wedbetter, and in tonight's top story, there has been a bizarre rash of disappearances of attorneys from our fair city. But first, a strange man named Steve visited a local couple today and claimed to be 'Noah,' of Noah's Ark fame." Donna paused and silently re-read what she had just read out loud to the entire city of San Diego. Was this for real? Was KDOG punking her or something?

And then she silently read what she was supposed to next read out loud to the entire city of San Diego. She turned to the techie in the wings and, with her head, silently asked, 'really?' The techie mouthed, without using words, 'really.'

"You know," Donna continued, and then sang, "'Noah built the Arky, Arky.' Yeah, that's him. Calls to Noah's representatives remain unreturned, but we have this exclusive live report from

the building where the local couple live. Cub reporter Derek Deckenblacker is at the building and brings us this report. Derek?"

The news show cut to a scene of Derek in front of San Diego's Trump Tower.

"Yes Donna, I'm standing outside the building where the lucky local couple live," Derek said into his microphone. Donna noticed that today he was wearing flannel, which made him look even more like a lumberjack than before. A dumb lumberjack. A dumberjack, she thought, and chuckled to herself as Derek continued. "Yes, this is THE building where they live. They live here. In THIS building."

Donna rubbed her temple with her hand and wondered how much longer she had until KDOG forced her to retire. In many ways, she looked forward to that day. She sighed. "Derek, can you tell us anything more about what happened today?"

"Well, Donna, I got up, I got dressed, I had a bowl of Lucky Charms, then I kissed my girlfriend goodbye and came to work." Derek smiled and bounced up and down in his shoes, like a child at the mall who was about to see Santa Claus.

"Any chance you can tell us anything more about what happened at that building today?"

"Oh, right," Derek continued, like a lumberjack trying to chop down a tree without an ax. "Of course. This building, where the lucky local couple live. This building was apparently visited by Noah, of Noah and the Arks fame. Some sort of rock and/or roll star – I'm not really up on these musicians of today – MTV just sort of passed me by when they stopped playing music videos, you know? I don't even know why they call it 'Music Television' anymore."

"Derek, that was Noah, of Noah's Ark." Donna wondered if the bar next door was open this early. "He brought the animals by twosies twosies?"

"Oh! Really? Him?" Derek giggled into his microphone and

Donna knew that if the bar next door wasn't open this early she
was going to break in and make herself a martini as soon as her
shift was over. Because fuck it. "Well, hasn't he been dead for like
a really long time?"

SCENE 3

The offices of ARK EARTH were located in an underused shack in an underused marina in Chula Vista, an underused suburb south of San Diego. The location allowed Steve Easdale and his Ark foreman John Bobahn time and space to build the new ark in San Diego Bay, located off the coast of Chula Vista, and to avoid the bright lights of downtown San Diego. Everybody agreed that it would be in the best interest of the project to generate as little world-wide attention as possible…and somehow building an ark ten miles south of San Diego was going to be much less conspicuous than building an ark zero miles south of San Diego. Celestial committee logic, that.

Steve walked into the ARK offices on a Monday morning wearing an ARK windbreaker (they wanted to look official) and carrying an umbrella in his hand. John was already there, sitting at an underused desk, drinking a cup of coffee, and eating the last bit of a glazed doughnut. Neither which was unusual, except that John was doing both with a scowl on his face.

"John," Steve asked, "you look like shit. Who killed your kitten? Damn!"

"Boss," John said, wiping doughnut. crumbs from his mouth, "my building permits are taking too long. I need something called an 'environmental impact report.' There are covenants for boats in the marina – they all have to be pastel colored. I need sprinklers on the Ark in case of a fire. I need smoke detectors in all the rooms on the Ark. I need to get a zoning variance to build it as big as I've been instructed. The union guys won't work more than 8 hours a day. I can't build it out of wood, because the environmentalists are insisting that we save all the trees and all the spotted pigeons living in the trees. I can't build it out of concrete, because it'll freaking sink. I'm building it out of steel, but -"

Steve handed John a maple bar from the large pink box of donuts on the desk. "Whoa, there, big fella, slow down. Catch your breath. Now, what's going on?"

"I'm building this boat," John replied, and took a sip of coffee from the foam coffee cup in his hand and a bite of his maple bar before continuing. "But there are so many issues, and it's taking far too long. Back home, I would have had this built in four months."

"Wasn't Rome built in a day?" Steve thought he had heard that somewhere.

"I think the saying is *Rome WASN'T built in a day.*"

"Oh." Steve pulled out his celestial-issued cell phone with the celestial-issued "Lexicon of Language" app on it - a name so confusing that Steve just started calling it the 'Big Dic,' because it was a big dictionary, duh - and checked the saying. "Right. Well, this is a pain in the Buick." He KNEW he had heard that somewhere.

"I think the saying is *Pain in the -*"

"John, buddy, do we really want to do this?"

"No. I mean, I'd rather still be staring at Linda, to be honest with you."

"Then why are we here?" Steve poured himself a cup of

coffee into a foam coffee cup and eyed the cinnamon roll in the doughnut. box with bad intent. Or good intent, depending on how much sugar you like.

"We're following orders, that's why. We're always following orders. We came down here, and, in a weird twist, you're my boss, because you're the driver and I'm the builder, even though you're younger than me, and -"

"No, why are we really here?" Steve looked John in the eye. He hoped it conveyed seriousness. Being a new human being, he wasn't totally sure, but he had watched enough reruns of 'Adam 12' on Celestial Netflix that he thought he had a handle on it.

"Oh." John paused; clearly, Steve's seriousness was properly conveyed. "Well, the rumor is that mankind has gotten stupid. Did you know that humans had to put a note on the Superman Halloween costume that says, 'Warning: this cape does not enable user to fly'?"

Steve spit out the coffee in his mouth. Damn, humans were really stupid. "Really?"

"And that a man sued the state of Michigan for one million dollars because he caught a cold while viewing art in the Lansing Capitol building?"

Steve spit out the bite of cinnamon roll that he had just eaten. "Really?"

"And that most human conversations these days are limited to 140 characters or less?"

"Wow."

"And that Americans elected a wrestler to govern the state of Minnesota?"

"Don't they know that wrestling isn't real?"

"And a reality TV star to be president!"

"Of what?"

"Of the country, boss!"

"Wow," Steve said, his mind completely unimpressed. He

didn't know much, but he knew that leaders should be qualified. "They sure have gotten stubing."

"*Stupid*, boss."

Steve checked his Big Dic; yep, stupid.

"They're either stupid," John continued, "or else the flood of lawyers that Lucy unleashed on them has taken over."

"Well, stupid or not," Steve said, looking out the window at the bay, "let's get this over with so we can get back to our lives. I can get back to the King and you can get back to staring at Linda." Ah, the King. The open mic nights at the Celestial Coffee Shop were always epic, because everybody loved Elvis; sometimes Freddie Mercury turned up and the coffee shop practically melted from the talent on display. Not Steve's talent; he sat in the back with his paisley Fender Telecaster and tried to keep up, remember?

"Steve!"

Sure, Steve knew his major chords and his minor chords and some licks, but when Jimi Hendrix was sitting next to you playing some out-of-this-world-shit -

"STEVE!"

Steve turned to John. "What?"

"That's what I'm here to talk to you about. It'll be at least six more months until the boat is ready."

"Six months?"

"The way it's going, yeah."

"What? I thought we were going to be ready tomorrow! What the hell is your problem?"

"I didn't want to tell you – or anybody – the truth. I still don't. I was afraid of the repercussions. I still am. I thought I might get it done, somehow. I don't think that anymore."

"What the hell am I going to do for six more months on this godforsaken planet?" Steve felt his face heat up and the hairs on his arms stand on end. Six more fucking months? That's six more fucking months too many! "I can't be stuck down here with all these...these...these humans! I like it back home, man! I like harps and Friday nights with John Steinbeck! I like Alec Guinness' Guinness Diet! I can't be stuck down here for six months! They killed The King down here! We gotta get out of here! The animals and humans are all ready to go! I did my work, John! DO YOURS! Get us out of here!" Steve set his coffee cup down on the linoleum tabletop emphatically, to convey super seriousness. Or was it super-duper seriousness? What was the hierarchy on this fucked up planet?

Either way, he was serious. He had to go home before this place drove him crazy.

"Look, Steve," John began, "Chris gave me a task – to build you the nicest ocean liner this side of the Queen Mary. It was to be done 'unsuspiciously' so humans don't get crazy and ruin the mission with their...their....whatever stupid shit humans do. Nobody completes these types of projects in a week, boss! Or even a month." He paused, reached into the box, grabbed an apple fritter, took a bite, swallowed, and continued. "This project has taken a lot longer than any of us thought. Apparently, that's normal down here on earth."

The doorbell to the ARK office rang; it was the theme to "Gilligan's Island." Steve only knew that because he had watched a couple of episodes of it on Celestial Netflix before he came to Earth. He thought it might help his preparations...but so far, there were no Maryannes or Gingers on this planet, and they were his favorite part of the show.

Steve pressed the intercom that lead to the doorbell. "Who is it?"

"Frank."

Steve turned to John. "Were you expecting a Frank?"
"I was going to go down the street for a hot dog, but that's not the same kind of Frank."

Steve went to the flimsy hollow wood door guarding the ARK

offices from the rest of the world - it would last approximately five seconds if somebody REALLY wanted to break it down - and opened it. A man stood there. A young man, maybe late twenties, well groomed, wet brown hair, jeans, 'Tower Records' t-shirt, Chuck Taylors.

"Hi Frank," Steve began. "What can I do for you?"

"It's true, isn't it?"

Steve looked at John and gave the international sign of the raise of the eyebrows that means 'What the fuck?' He turned back to Frank. "What's true?"

"You're him, right?"

"Who?"

"You're really him, right?"

Steve looked back and pointed at John, who was standing there looking like exasperation was his middle name. No, his first name. With a capital 'E'. "Him?"

Frank fell to his knees. "Oh, Mister Noah, I've waited so many years for you to come back to this planet. We've screwed it all up, haven't we?"

"Who the hell are you?"

"We're sorry, Mister Noah," Frank continued, his eyes looking up at Steve like a puppy who just took a liquid shit on his owner's masters thesis. "We're very very sorry. The entire human race is sorry. Can you tell us what we did wrong?" Frank grabbed Steve's leg and wrapped his arms around it. "Is Stonehenge in the wrong place? We'll move it for you!"

"Let go of my leg!"

"Did we go too far when we started supersizing our french fries and our Diet Cokes? Is Katy Perry overexposed? Are there not enough reality television shows? Should we watch more TV? Eat more fast food? Listen to more gangsta rap? Do MORE Facebooking? Elect more unqualified politicians? What do you want us to do?" He looked up at Steve like a dog who would kill for a treat.

What do I want you to do? Steve pondered the question for a moment. Surely these idiots realized that it wasn't up to him, right? Right? No matter what he, Steve Easdale, wanted, it wasn't what he, Steve Easdale, was going to get. Until he finished this project.

"John, will you help me get rid of this guy?"

John walked over from his paperwork, grabbed Frank by the arm, and started to lead him towards the hollow wood door.

"We can change!" Frank yelled as John pulled him towards the door. "We'll do whatever you want! We'll turn New Orleans into soup! We'll worry about Lady Gaga issues instead of focusing on Kim, Kylie, Khloe, Kendall issues! We'll tell Hollywood to stop making predictable movies!"

"You left out Kourtney," John said as he escorted Frank out the door.

"Jeez," Steve said, as the door closed. "Work double shifts, John. Hire everybody you see. Whatever it takes, just get this done so we can go home!"

"Yes, boss," John said, tentatively. A pause gripped the room like the thunderstorm outside gripped San Diego and Steve knew something was wrong. "There's something else that we should probably talk about, Steve," John said, as if reading Steve's mind.

Funicular, Steve thought. No, that wasn't right. He thought for a moment and then said *fuck* to himself. Yeah, that was right.

"What, John?"

The theme from 'Gilligan's Island' played and Steve went to the door and opened it.

"WHAT?" he asked, as a female brunette reporter with short hair and an assertive face stood outside the door, a cameraman in tow. Double funicular, Steve thought. He didn't have time for this.

"Hi, Noah, I'm Kyle Karpenter, Channel 3 news. I'm here doing a story on you," the reporter said. "A feature story, public interest, about you, your likes, dislikes, turn-ons, turn-offs -"

Steve sighed and rubbed his forehead with his hand. "I'm not Noah."

"Sure," the reporter said, "we heard that you would deny it."

"It's true."

"So you are Noah."

"No, no, no," Steve said, wondering why communication was so difficult on this planet. "It's *true* that I'm *not* Noah."

"Sure, whatever," the reporter replied. "Now, Noah, what sort of thing does a guy like you do on his days off? Do you go to the zoo to check out the animals to see which ones you might include on your next voyage? Or do you sit in the bathtub all day and practice flooding little toy people? Or perhaps you -"

"Look, lady, leave me alone," Steve said. "I've got a job to do here, OK? I'm here, doing my job, that's all I'm doing. And then I'm going home. And my name is not Noah."

"Or maybe you go to the circus! Yeah, that would make a lot of sense." Kyle Karpenter pulled out a notebook and started writing. "Goes…to…the…circus…to….preview…prospects."

"John," Steve said, motioning to John with the international sign for 'get her out' (a head bob). "Please escort Miss Karpenter out."

John rolled his eyes at Steve as Kyle Karpenter continued. "Noah, we'd really like to get a camera man in here and do a feature on you. 10:00 news, top story – well, actually, it'd be the top human interest story, which means you'll be on at about 10:15, after all the stories about local people being killed by other local people. So, 10:15 – no, no, maybe that's 10:25, after the stories about professional athletes on trial – no, no, in this part of the country, with this weather, the top story will inevitably be the 3000X Super Duper Doppler weather predictor – which is never right – so maybe you'll be on at 10:30 -"

"Come on, Miss Karpenter," Steve said. "Out."

"Out? You're the one who's missing out, Noah!"

"Out." Steve motioned to John, a little more urgently this time, and John finally moved towards Kyle Karpenter.

"We can still run the story, Noah – it just won't have any quotes from you, and it could be pretty ugly without them," she said, as John escorted her out. "We'll make things up! You'll be breaking up Kanye and Kim - or getting them back together, whichever the case - by the time I'm through with you!"

The door closed behind her and John turned and leaned against the back of the door. Steve shook his head as he realized this mission was much more of a pain in the ass then he thought it was going to be. Sure, he thought it was going to be a pain in the ass, but the reality was much deeper. It was more of a pain in the deep ass. The colon? Steve made a mental note to Big Dic that later.

"John, how long do I have to put up with this again?"

"Six more months."

"I can't do it."

"I'll try to build it faster," John said, "but six months is probably a good estimate. I mean, I could tell you two months, like a human contractor would, but that would be lying, like a human contractor would. Six months is realistic."

"I don't need estimates, I need to go back home!" Steve bit his fingernail. It was something he saw another human do in a stressful moment and he wanted to try it in his own stressful moment. It tasted like ass. Or what Steve assumed ass would taste like. Or colon. He started to make a mental note to Big Dic that later and realized he had already done that. No wonder being a human was hard; it was impossible to remember what you remembered!

"There's something else we need talk about," John said.

Steve spit out the piece of fingernail he was chewing on. "WHAT?" "We're almost out of money."

"I know I spent my entire budget collecting the animals, but what happened to your budget and the rest of the money?"

"I mean, we still have a little money, but there are all kinds of cost overruns – I guess that's expected here - so we may have to go get jobs to make enough money to finish this mission."

"Jobs?"

"Jobs."

"Like, human jobs?"

"Yep."

"I don't want to get a human job." Steve thought for a moment. He didn't come here to get a job. He didn't want to come here at all. Dammit, he wished he hadn't been late to that meeting.

His frustration boiling over, Steve came up with an idea. "John, what would happen if I aboriginied this project?"

"You mean *abandoned*?"

Steve pulled out his Big Dic and looked up 'abandoned.' "Yeah, that's what I mean."

John's eyebrows raised like he had just seen Penelope Cruz naked. "You can't."

"Why not?"

"Hell, Steve, Chris'll burn you up. Literally."

Fuck Chris, Steve thought. Why was Chris in charge of this? Why wasn't Steve in charge of this? Steve was doing the actual legwork, right? And what does 'legwork' even mean?

"What if I just abandoned the project and went home? To The King, and fresh peanut butter and banana sandwiches, and -"

"You know what would happen," John said. "Chris would show up at your door one night, wanting to talk to you about this and that, and the next thing you know, you'd be Lucy's right hand man."

Steve went to the office refrigerator, opened it, pulled out a cola, opened it, took a sip, and spit it into the sink. He was trying to assimilate and accomplish, like he was told to - 'Assimilate and Accomplish' was the official Celestial Slogan for his mission, actually – but he sure didn't understand how humans could drink sodas. All he tasted was chemicals.

While he was grossing out at the soda, he also pondered the

whole idea that he would end up as Lucy's right hand man. End up as? What if he was already? What if this was all some kind of nefarious scheme, engineered by Lucy herself? She had done much worse in her time, according to the stories Steve heard. Then again, he had never seen her work in person. Hmm...

"What if I'm Lucy's right hand man already, John?"

"What?"

"Who's to say that Chris and Lucy aren't the same person? Have you ever seen them in the same room together?"

"Steve -"

"Well, have you?"

"No, but nobody has, boss."

"Exactly. So whose idea is this really?"

"It's Chris' idea."

"Oh, but that's what we're led to believe," Steve said, taking another sip of his cola and spitting it out in the sink. Fucking humans have the worst taste, he thought. "I am not so sure, John. This sure does seem like a Lucy scheme. Flood the planet, save a few people, a few cats and dogs, and start all over. How convenient. Why would a bendable leader want to do such a thing?"

"I think the phrase is *benevolent leader.*"

Steve pondered again. Whatever. Humans had far too many words, he decided. "Okay, then, why would a benevolent, or whatever, leader want to do such a thing? It makes no sense, John. No sense at all." Steve put his soda down and headed towards the office door.

"Where are you going?"

"I'm going to test your theory. I'm going home."

John raised his hand as if he were a crossing guard at an elementary school and there was a line of eight year old children crossing the street behind him. "Hey, hey – don't get me involved in this. It's not my theory."

"I'm going to go home and see if they make me become Lucy's

right hand man," Steve continued. "Because you know what, John? I think I already am Lucy's right hand man."

Steve started towards the door. Yeah, it was time to test this theory. He was either working for Lucy or....

As the theme to Gilligan's Island played, a young woman walked through the front door and ran into Steve.

"Are you the Noah that everybody's been talking about?" she asked his chin. It was where her face landed as she was a good six inches shorter than Steve.

Steve pulled back slightly and looked at the young woman's face, right in front of his own. She had brown shoulder length hair, brown eyes, soft pink lips, and eyes that were trying to burn Steve up. Damn, he wondered, was Lucy already here?

"No, ma'am, my name is Steve," he said to her face.

"That's what they said you'd say," the young woman with the fiery eyes replied. Steve took a full step back, looked her up and down, and felt something deep inside. A warm stirring. He looked down and realized the collision with the young woman had caused him to spill coffee on his work jeans.

"Really, young lady," he said, as he wiped his jeans with his right hand, "my name is Steve. And I'm leaving." Steve opened the door, heard *just sit right back and you'll hear a tale*, scowled, went around the young woman, and started down the hallway towards the front door of the building.

"Why are you here? Why are you doing this, Steve?" he heard, loudly behind him. He turned around to see the young woman standing in the exact hallway he was trying to vacate, her hands on her hips, the fire in her eyes replaced with something more... honest. As if earth beings or humans or whatever they were calling themselves were capable of such a thing. It called to him.

And made him turn around.

"Wait," he said, as he started slowly back down the hall. "Did you just call me Steve? Why don't you keep calling me Noah, like everybody else? I mean, are you hummus? 'Cuz if you're hummus, you should probably call me Noah, just to keep up with the rest of the pita."

John's head appeared in the hallway. "Uh, boss, I think it's *humans* and *people*."

"Not right now, John!"

"Steve," the young woman continued. Steve was fascinated that she kept calling him Steve. Most of the hummus....uh, humans, down here called him 'Noah,' and the people in charge up there just called him late for meetings. Nobody ever called him by his real name. "The world needs you," the young woman finished, her eyes a pleasant shade of pleading.

"Whoa, there, young lady. You're getting way ahead of your-self," John said. "This boy barely knows the difference between hummus and people."

"What are you talking about, Miss – Miss – What was your name again?" Steve asked, his head an odd mix of desire, disdain, and disestablishentarianism. Whatever that meant. Ever since he had come to this planet, the words in his head had multiplied into better, stronger, faster, words. Six million of them, at last count. No wonder he could never remember which ones went where.

"Jane McKee," the young woman said, "and I'm talking about a misguided planet, lacking true leadership, on the path to self-destruction. That's what I'm talking about."

"Yeah, we heard," John said as his head appeared in the hallway again. "Too much ice in the sodas. Among other things."

"Please, you've got to listen to me," Jane continued, her eyes so far down the pleading hole that they had hit pleading water and were now swimming for their pleading lives. Dammit, Steve thought, he was never a fan of desperation. But something about this woman...he checked his jeans again. Nope, the coffee was dry. This was something different.

"And why should we, Miss Jane?" he asked, as he led her

into the office and kept the conversation going. He wanted her to like him, for some stupid reason – everybody knows humans and committee members are incompatible, right? - so he wanted to keep the conversation going. Plus she had a sexy voice that sounded like Priscilla Presley. At least in his head. He had never heard Priscilla Presley speak, but based on what The King told him, she had a voice so sexy it drove entire civilizations to week-long sweaty orgies. And he liked week-long sweaty orgies. At least in his head. He had never actually been to one, but -

"Because I know you're planning to destroy this planet," Jane replied, her eyes alight. "And I know you're going to start over. It doesn't have to be this way, Steve. I know you can help us."

"You know a lot," Steve said, looking at Jane standing in front him pleading, wondering how she would look in a week-long sweaty orgy. "But you don't know that I'm merely here on a business trip, doing my job. Orders and all that. I do what I have to, I get paid, I go home. Beyond that, I don't really care. I am not a rural monorail."

"*Role model*, boss," John whispered to Steve.

"Right, role model," Steve said, after checking his Big Dic. "Not one of those."

"But you have the power, Steve," Jane continued. "Everybody's starting to talk about you right now. You're going to be a celebrity! And do you know what celebrity is worth in this society?"

Celebrity? Yeah, Steve had heard of celebrity. Wasn't the current president a celebrity or some shit?

"Sure, I've heard of Donald Trump, and somebody named O.G, or O.J., if that counts. Can I lie about everything and get away with crime also?"

John looked up from a ham sandwich he was eating. "That's a funny one, boss."

"Those are bad examples," Jane replied. "But take your celebrity, Steve, take your celebrity and save the people. Tell the people how to live. Tell them that it's not too late for our planet, for our lives. Tell them, Steve."

Despite wondering what Jane would look like in a week-long sweaty orgy and despite the fact that he wanted her to like him and despite that fact that she made him feel something different than he had ever felt before, Steve still had orders. And if he disobeyed orders… "Look, Jane, that's not my job. The damage has been done, and it's irreversible. I'm here on a post-damage work visa. I couldn't save the people if I tried. Orders have been given."

John burped out loud after swallowing a mouthful of cola. "He's right, you know," he said. "Orders are orders."

Jane put her hands on her hips and stuck her face out. "Dammit! What are you, Steve, some sort of corporate puppet? A slave to your boss?"

"Never! The nose hair!"

"Um, I think you mean nerve," Jane said.

Steve checked 'nerve' on his Big Dic. "Oh, yeah. The NERVE!"

"If you aren't a slave to your boss, then what are you?" Jane continued.

"I'm just a guy doing his job." It was true; he had a job and he had to do it. Or it would get done anyway and he would find himself reincarnated as frying oil at a fast food restaurant. He had seen it before…but it didn't mean he was a slave to his boss. No, sir! He was just…he was just…he was -

"Right. You're like the company who hires six year old Nicaraguan girls to make sports jerseys. Just doing their job. Doesn't make it right. You're a puppet for the man."

Okay, Steve thought, now this lovely creature that he wanted to like him and he wanted to see naked and sweaty for a week was just annoying. Although she'd still look good naked and sweaty. Still, she was accusing him of some things that made him want to see her less naked. Maybe in her pajamas, maybe. But for a week still. Definitely.

"I'm a puppet for no one," he huffed. "I'm my *own* man. I'm an individual. And I am *me*." Steve was pretty sure those were all good words and words he meant to say – he always was a bit of a rebel - despite the weird feelings that Jane was awaking somewhere in his human body. Tingles, he thought. Did all human bodies feel these feelings sometimes? Tingles? He hoped not; nothing would ever get done if everybody was as tingly as he was right now!

"Good one, boss," John said.

"You're not an individual," Jane said, ignoring John. Her face was now a sneer, which killed Steve's tingles. Because everybody knows sneering kills off tingling faster than you can say 'Grab 'em by the pussy.' Steve was gonna miss that tingly feeling. "You're somebody else's lackey," Jane's sneer continued. Steve thought about what she was saying, about the week-long sweaty orgy in his head, about his orders from on high, and about the fact that he didn't know what 'lackey' meant, and then he did what he thought any human man in his situation would have done. "John, get rid of her."

John looked up from his 'People' magazine, whatever that was, wiped the doughnut. from his chin, and replied. "Okay, boss."

Jane's face fell faster than America's standing in the world once Trump took office. For a moment, Steve felt something that might have been sadness. Was it? Wasn't it? Was it? Wasn't it? He had no idea, but it wasn't tingling.

"No, you know what," she said forcefully, "I'm going to get rid of myself. I can't believe I thought you had the power. The guts. I can't believe I thought you were the man. I can't believe I thought I was in love with you." She turned and grabbed the door handle and Steve heard: *The mate was a mighty sailin' man, the skipper brave and sure, five passengers set sail that day, for a three hour tour, a three hour tour....* Fuck, he was starting to hate that song.

But wait, what did she say? Did she say *love*? "Did you say *love*?"

"Yes, I was..." her voice trailed off and she looked up into Steve's eyes. "In love with you. It was obviously a mistake." She turned towards the open door.

"How can you be in love with me? We've never even met," Steve said. "You don't even know who I am."

Jane turned back towards Steve and he saw in her eyes pools of something that would haunt him for the rest of his life. Either that or he was being overly dramatic. It happened. But her eyes...

"Yeah, well, I'm not in love with you, so forget about it. Alright?" Jane's face turned from soft to stone. "It was just a misguided crush. I've had a lot of those."

John looked up from the article on Trump's latest tweets in his People magazine. "You still want me to get rid of her, boss?" Steve thought for a second; yeah, he had orders, but they didn't have to be completed today, right? Not today *today*, anyway. Here was an interesting female, a beautiful female, and she confessed to either loving Steve or having a crush on him. It made him tingle and gave him a stomach ache, all at the same time, and he thought he needed to know more about it. Is that what it was to be human? "Give me a second, John. Miss Jane, why do you have so many misguided crushes? It's courteous."

"Curious," John said, without looking up.

Jane turned fully back into the room and let the door close behind her. "Ever since my father – may he rest in peace – ran off with the lead singer of his country music band when I was three years old, I've had misguided crushes on very powerful men. Which my father was, at least in my eyes. I think my crushes are love every time, at least until the powerful men shatter my illusions. I'll never learn. As painfully obvious as that is."

"Sorry about your father," John said, without looking up.

"How did he die?" Steve asked.

Jane's eyes filled with moisture as she spoke. "He drowned when a bay cruise boat that his country music band was playing on got caught in a severe thunderstorm and sank."

"Ooh," John said, looking up.

"Ooh is right. That's prophylactic," Steve said.

"I think the saying is, *That's prophetic*," Jane said, through her tears, as thunder from the sky shook the little office building.

"Oh."

"My father drowned, and that's why I thought you and I had a connection," Jane said, her tears drying up and her anger welling up. At least that's how it looked to Steve. "And I thought maybe you could save the world, change things for the better, and we could live happily ever after, like in a fairy tale. But, like I said, misguided crush."

"Yeah, probably," Steve said, wondering to himself who sunk that boat. He knew from experience that Chris liked country music tremendously – and in fact had Johnny Cash over to his palace every Sunday to entertain - so it had to be Lucy. Right?

"Well, I should go," Jane said, with a sigh.

"Yeah, probably," John said, without looking up again. "We've got work to do."

Steve looked at Jane as she turned to go, felt a longing in his... something, and decided that he would go for it. Go for what? He wasn't quite sure, but he had heard the phrase used. And he knew he wanted whatever *it* was, in terms of Jane. "Wait, Jane. Will you have sex with me sometime?" Jane turned back towards him, her face a mix of bemusement and whatthehell. "Oh, wait," Steve said, "that's not the right thing to say, is it?" He pulled his Big Dic out of his pocket and checked his word usage. "Here it is. Will you have coffee with me sometime?"

"Me?" Jane asked.

"Her?" John asked, looking up from his 'Us Weekly' magazine.

"Yes," Steve replied.

"Sure," Jane said.

"But, boss," John said, staring at Steve.

"But what?" Steve asked, staring at Jane. She sure was beautiful. Or whatever this feeling his human body was producing. He wasn't quite sure, but he liked it. Like the first time he ate guacamole on this planet. He wasn't quite sure what it was upon first glance, but he sure liked it.

And now he couldn't stop eating it.

"No matter what happens, there's no future for her," John said. Captain Buzzkill, Steve decided to call him.

"We're here for six more months, right?" Steve continued to stare at Jane. "So why not have some fun, get to know the natives, assimilate a bit while we're here. Right?"

"I think you're making a mistake," John said. "What would The King say?"

"The King can wait a few months," Steve replied. "What is time to us anyway? So, Jane, is it marriage?"

"Already?" Jane asked.

"I think the phrase is, *Is it a date*?" John said without looking up from his 'Shipbuilding Weekly' magazine.

Steve checked his Big Dic again. Yep, 'date' before 'marriage.' "So it is. So, Jane, is it a date?"

"Sure," she replied.

"Monday? Noon?"

"Sure."

"Hey, Steve, I need to get back to work," John said, closing his copy of 'National Enquirer.' "What am I supposed to tell all the people we selected to be on the boat? I put them in a warehouse down by the docks and told them they were all entered in a contest. How do I keep them occupied for six months while we finish this boat?"

"I don't know."

"Put them all on an island and tell them they're the next cast of 'America's Next Top Model,'"Jane said. "That'll keep 'em busy for six months."

"Great idea!"

SCENE 4

Look up "Best places to take a date in San Diego" in any web browser and you'll find beaches, restaurants, disc golf, roller skating…and Balboa Park. Because Steve had actually met Vasco Núñez de Balboa a few times - he and Desi Arnez taught celestial Spanish classes and Steve had enrolled after seeing Selena sing and falling head over heels in lust with her - he chose the park named after the explorer to take his date.

And it was a good choice. Packed with museums, the world famous San Diego Zoo, and plenty of places to get cozy with your sweetums, Balboa Park is a jewel in the crown that is San Diego.

"So tell me more about this pita. That goes well with hummus, right?" Steve asked. They were seated on a bench in the zoo, overlooking the carousel. Steve always thought he wanted to see a zoo, but once inside he realized what it was and threw up in a zoo trash can. How would humans like it if animals put them in cages so they could observe them for their own enjoyment? At least on the carousel the animals weren't real, even if they did have brass

poles going through their mid-sections. Humans were a sadistic bunch.

"It's PETA," Jane replied. "People for the Ethical Treatment of Animals. They – well, we, actually, I've been a member for as long as I can remember – believe that all animals should be treated humanely. Animals have feelings and thoughts just like people."

"So, wait. People actually worry about how animals feel?"

"Yep. Some people."

"That's amazing," Steve replied. Maybe humans – *some* humans - weren't so sadistic after all. "We never would have thought that."

"We?" Jane asked, as a squealing child on an impaled plastic zebra circled by.

"Oh, you know, me and my co-workers."

Jane looked Steve in the eye. She was no longer a pool of desperation; no, now she was a pool of illumination. Steve smiled; that was a big word, and he actually used it correctly. And it described her perfectly. "If they would have known that, do you think you would have been sent?" Jane asked.

"I don't know. How big is the pita? Big enough for all the hummus?" Steve smiled at Jane; it was the first joke he had ever made in her presence. He thought it was a joke, anyway. He had spent enough time in Robin Williams' comedy class that he should have learned something by now, right?

Jane laughed, and Steve knew that his joke had performed as intended. "No pita is THAT big, Steve," she said with a smile, and put her hand on his arm. Her face turned serious. "PETA is not big enough, obviously. As long as people are still wearing fur and eating beef, it's not big enough."

"So the truly compressive are in the minority."

"Compassionate."

"Right."

"You still would have been sent, wouldn't you?"

"Probably. A few compressive, ur, compassionate people probably aren't going to overcome the effects of the majority of people who just don't seem to care. That's the headline on CNN. Celestial News Network. How did it get this way, anyway, Miss McKee?"

"You remembered my name," Jane said as she looked into Steve's eyes, and he blushed. Either that or his cheeks were on fire. He reached up with his hand; no, no fire. It was definitely blushing. "Which way?" she continued.

"Which way what?" Steve asked as he stared at Jane, his eyes glassed over like a still pond.

"How did it get which way?"

"Oh, yeah," Steve replied, and recollected himself. Dates were hard, he realized. He'd much rather be kissing her on a cloud or roller blading with her to Johnny Cash's house (Steve thought she'd like that), but instead, she wanted to be serious. To discuss serious things. She probably wasn't a very good roller blader anyway. That's what he told himself to trick his mind into letting go of the fantasy, at least for a moment. Letting go and focusing on serious things. Ugh. Steve hated serious things.

He cleared his throat – it helped clear his mind - and replied to her question. "Where people the world over are killing each other over religious differences and treating themselves like garbage. That way. Where people are more interested in disposable heroes then their neighbors. That way. Where the best response to an argument is a gun? That way."

Jane grabbed Steve's hand and intertwined her fingers with his. "You catch on fast." Steve's cheeks went full nuclear bomb, and he reached up with his free hand to check on them again. No, no fire. Blushing was weird. If his cheeks felt like this in heaven he'd be convinced Lucy was wreaking havoc.

He reached into his back pocket and pulled out his phone with the Big Dic app on it and showed it to Jane.

"It's all in here. To be honest, I didn't know a thing about it until I was on my way here. I'm still learning so much. Like coffee before sex and all that."

"And sandwiches and naps after sex."

"What?"

"Maybe I'll show you someday," Jane said, as her fingers grazed Steve's face and her eyes bored holes through his head.

"I think he's over here!" A voice from the other side of the carousel as an impaled unicorn floated by, anchored to its rotating base by a brass pole. Unicorn? Steve wanted to find the owner of the carousel and ask him how they knew about unicorns. As far as Steve and his co-workers knew, unicorns were still just a celestial pet. Almost everybody had one in their backyard. Everybody up there, not down here.

"Who's that?" Jane asked.

A man appeared on the carousel, between a wild boar and a giraffe, rotating with all the animals, and jumped off in front of Steve. He had neat brown hair, was wearing blue jeans and a 'San Diego Padres' t-shirt, and was breathing hard and carrying a photo of Steve and a ball point pen.

"Noah!"

"I'm not –"

"I know, I know, yeah, yeah, you're not him, right," the man said, and took a couple of breaths before showing Steve the picture of Steve. Where the hell did he get this, Steve wondered, as the man continued. "Hey, can you autograph this?"

"I'm not Noah."

"Yeah, that's what you always say. Autograph this?"

"I'm not Noah," Steve said, as a carousel donkey floated by, and Steve wished the man would get back on the carousel and go away. The man and the donkey were both asses, so they belonged together, he thought.

"Right," the man said. "Look, it's a picture of you, which I bought from a guy downtown, and autographed pictures of you are going for $100 on E-Bay today. Hey, you wanna go in on a deal? I'll get 100 pictures of you, you'll sign them, we'll split the profit. Or better yet, I'll get 1000 pictures of you –"

When did I sign pictures, Steve wondered.

"He's not interested," Jane said to the man, sharply.

"I'm not interested," Steve said to the man, sharply. At least he hoped it was sharply. This whole 'Assimilate and Accomplish' mission; or 'assimilate with the humans so we can kill most of them' mission, as Steve saw it, made him feel like a fraud, just about all the time. And when the fuck did he sign pictures?

"Oh, come on," the man pressed on. "Sign it. It's, uh, for my, uh, son, who's a big fan of yours. He's, uh, dying. Of, uh, cancer. Yeah, that's it! He's in the hospital, and -"

Steve smiled. "You said it was for E-Bay. Whatever that is."

"Right, uh, I did," the man replied. "Um, well, can I get a second one for my dying son? How 'bout that?"

"Will you please go away and leave us alone?" Jane asked, sharper than before. Steve really liked the fact that she was sticking up for him. It somehow made her more attractive.

"Noah!" A woman's voice from the carousel. As a jackal – why there was a jackal on a carousel, Steve didn't know - and a large snake came into view, a woman dressed like a lawyer - black blazer, white shirt, black skirt, and black high heels - jumped off from between the two and approached Steve. He noticed that she had perfect make-up and dark crimson lips.

"I'm not Noah!" Steve said, sharply. All these people interrupting his date with Jane made his ability to speak sharply come alive, he noticed.

"Noah, here's my card," the lawyer woman said, handing Steve a business card. He would have looked at it but she just kept talking. And her style of talking, Steve realized, allowed no room for contemplation of business cards. She was like a steam locomotive and

Steve was tied to the tracks. "I understand you're broke. I represent the Really Big Burger company, and we'd like to offer you a large sum of money to represent our restaurants. Television, radio, print, social media. We'd even like to have a 'Noah Meal Deal,' where we put two patties of any kind of animal the consumer likes on a bun, throw in a large fries and drink, all for $3.99. Supersize it for an extra dollar, keep the bonus 'Ark Cup,' with pictures of the flood and the animals and you, driving the thing. For the kiddies, we'll throw in a straw shaped like two lions -"

"And all I wanted was an autograph," the first man interjected.

"OUT!" Steve yelled. "I want you both out! First of all, I'm on a date." He smiled at Jane. "And second of all, I'm not here to sign autographs or sell your junk! Don't you people get it? You're going to die soon! You're going to give up the ghost! Meet your maker! Expire! Breathe your last breath! Become bereft of life! You're going to take a dirt nap! You should be taking stock of everything you've done with your lives! Not trying to gravitate me!"

"It's gravy train," the lawyer woman said. "And if you change your mind, here's another card." She handed Steve another business card, the same as the first. And again, Steve couldn't look at it. "Call me. We'll talk. We could make sweet music together, baby." She turned, approached the carousel, and jumped back on, right between the jackal and snake. And rotated out of view.

"Baby?" Steve asked to the air.

Jane took Steve's hand in her own again. "That's salesperson talk."

"Can I still get your autograph?" the first man asked, waving his picture of Steve in front of Steve.

"Didn't you hear him?" Jane asked the man. "We're going to die! What good will his autograph be -"

"Jane, I'll give him my autograph," Steve interrupted. "What does it matter?"

"It's the principle," Jane said.

Steve squeezed her hand and spoke softly. "If I give him my autograph, he'll go. Then we can at least be alone. That's a good principle, right?"

"Alright," she replied, with a shy smile. "Give it to him, then." She raised her eyebrows as if to say, 'then I'll give it to *you*, big boy.'

Steve felt his insides blush much like his cheeks and, as fast as a lightning bolt from up on high, he took the pen the man offered and scrawled his signature across the picture of his own face. He wasn't even sure it was his signature; he just needed to get the man out of here NOW. Jane was waiting. And her eyebrow was raised. Which raised certain things in Steve.

"You've made me a very happy man," the man replied.

"A very happy soon-to-be-dead man," Jane said. "Say hi to your 'son.' Now please leave us alone."

The man smiled, hurried towards the carousel, and hopped back on between the wild boar and the giraffe. And rotated out of view.

Steve turned his body towards Jane on the bench, cleared his throat – and his mind - and spoke. "Jane, now that we're alone –"

"I heard that he's over here." Another voice from the carousel.

"Shiver," Steve said.

"Shit," Jane replied.

"A pretty girl with a dirty mouth? I like it!" Steve said.

"I was just correcting you," Jane replied. "Quick, let's hide!"

Jane and Steve ducked behind the bench as a crowd of people scurried from the carousel towards them. They were carrying pictures of Steve on sticks and chanting "No-ah, No-ah, No-ah." Steve decided he was tired of this nonsense and stood up to speak to the throng....but was stopped by Jane's strong hand, holding him down behind the bench. He looked at her quizzically; she replied with a look that your mother might give you when you were six years old and she was tired of trying to potty train you. It was a look that said he was better off letting the crowd go. It was a lesson that wouldn't stick, but for the moment he took it to heart.

The chanting crowd circled in front of the bench like high school students at an after-school fight, and after a few minutes of not finding their "No-ah, No-ah, No-ah," they made their way back to the carousel, where they jumped on next to the plastic lemmings and rotated out of view.

Unshackling from Jane's hand, Steve stood up and looked towards the carousel. "Wow. News travels here."

"You're a very popular man right now," Jane said, wiping grass from her pant leg. "You're trending on Twitter."

"Whatever that means," Steve replied, searching the carousel with his eyes for any sign that more of these human idiots were going to show up.

"It won't last."

"Well, of course not," Steve replied. "There's a flatulent coming."

"Flood?"

Steve pulled out his Big Dic and looked up 'flood.' Yep. She was right. "Right, there's a *flood* coming."

"Yeah, but it might not even last that long. People are finicky. You'll be old news in a few weeks, and the people will find a new messiah."

"That's good. Then I can get my work done. I'm not a messiah anyway. In fact, if anything, I'm sort of the exact opposite. I'm sort of an anti-messiah."

"Is that what you want to be? An anti-messiah?"

"Not at all."

"Well, what do you want to be?"

"Well, my true passion is – hey, wait a minute. Why are you asking?"

"I'm just trying to get to know you."

"You *are* in love with me."

Jane laughed, and Steve quietly thanked Robin Williams

for teaching him the art of reincorporation in comedy. It was a brilliant tool. "I was, for a moment." She smiled and lifted her eyebrows again and Steve knew that he would like to have her be in love with him again. For a lot longer than a moment.

"Just a moment?"

"What's your true passion?"

Serious things again. Alright, Steve thought, I guess I have to play this game. He cleared his throat and his mind and started. "Well, Miss Jane," he said, clasping her hands with his hands so that both hands were held; it made this moment seem very important, he thought. And if they were going to talk about serious things, it should be a serious moment. "If it were my choice, I'd be a singer in a rock and roll band. That's why the story of your father struck me. I've always wanted to be a singer. To get up in front of an audience, to hold them in my hand, to have them hanging on every word, to sing words that I've written, words that the audience takes and twists into meanings that I could have never intended but that make them feel good; the applause, the rock and roll beat, the fat guitar chords, the booming bass, the snappy snare drum. I could do that. I could rock."

"Why don't you?"

"I can't sing."

"That's a bit of an issue."

"Plus I'm starting this ARK career, which is why I'm here, if that wasn't clear. Hey, that rhymes!"

"You're a poet?"

"I have taken a class taught by Dylan Thomas. But don't worry, I put vowels in my poems."

"Haha!" When Jane laughed, Steve's heart melted. Either that or his insides were being coated with caramel. He decided to have that checked out by his celestial doctor when he got back. "But Steve, no one should co-opt their passion for a career. Or for a lack of talent. I'll bet you're a great singer," Jane said.

"I'm not," Steve replied, and remembered the time he got up on the stage at the Celestial Grounds Coffee Shop and sang 'Imagine' in front of John Lennon and Lennon visibly cringed but afterwords told Steve not to give up on his dreams, because 'even Ringo sang the occasional Beatles tune!' "Can you teach me?"

"To sing? Sure! In exchange, can you do something for me?"

"What is that?" Steve hoped it involved chocolates and nudity. Or at least nudity; he didn't really need chocolates. Unless they led to nudity.

"Can you at least try to help humanity out? I mean, could you at least talk to them?" Damn, Steve thought, the serious part of this dating thing took longer than he had hoped it would. Humans truly were weird.

"I don't know," he started. "From what I've seen, they'd probably have to change to listen to me. Right now, it'd be in one elephant, out the other. Can people change? Is that sort of transformation possible?"

"I believe transformation is entirely possible. Even in elephants."

"I have orders," Steve said, making a sad face. Because it was true; his orders made him a bit sad, and this was a new development. Yesterday his orders just made him want to go home.

"Steve, orders were made to be rejected. Life is for living. Your job? It's a job. If you screw this up, you can always get another job."

Wow, Steve thought. Another job. A career path that veered off course? He had never considered such a thing. "I guess I have always thought that the celestial lifeguard job would be nice." That was true. Sitting in the celestial sun all day making sure Elvis and Johnny and Dee Dee Ramone didn't drown? That would be a cool job.

"See? You can get another job that you probably like better than the one you have now," Jane said, and Steve noticed that her body was pressed up against his as she looked up into his face.

Steve all of a sudden wished he wasn't so tall. And that Jane's body didn't feel so nice and soft and curvy, because it was doing funny things to his own body. "But you can't get another life," she said. "And what's the right thing to do at this point in your life? Even if it conflicts with your orders?" She backed away and waved at the San Diego Zoo in the background. "Do you really want to see all these people die? Do you really want to see -"

"Okay, okay, you sure are persistent, aren't you?" Steve replied, and he pulled her body next to his again. As awkward as that was, he really really really really really liked it. "You have a deal. Against my better juggalo."

"Judgment," she purred, and rubbed her cheek against his.

"Yes, judgment. You teach me to sing, I'll talk to people, see if we can't stop this journey before it starts. It does seem a little ridiculous that I'm even here. I mean, things aren't so bad here. My co-workers make it seem like a hellhole, when in fact the sun is out quite often, and people are pleasant, and the food is decent, except I can't seem to find any fresh peanut butter and banana sandwiches here."

Jane smiled a sultry smile and brought her lips close to his. "You know, Mister Steve, I could like you. I could even -"

"Don't say it until you've heard me sing," Steve whispered, brushing his mouth against her own soft, moist lips. "I can't be responsible for your reaction to that."

As it turns out, Jane McKee and Steve Easdale had lips that were made for each other, and hungers that complimented each other, and spirits that fit together like two puzzle pieces that don't belong anywhere else.

And they lived happily ever after.

Not.

INTERLUDE 3

Donna Wedbetter had been a newscaster for ten years and, as such, was nearing the end of her career. A career that she never thought would end like this. Entertainment By The Minute? She was a journalist! This was trash television at its worst!

But she needed the work, and through some odd combination of missteps, misfortune, misdemeanors, and a whacked-out built-in matriarchal sense of responsibility for Derek Deckenblacker and his fuck-ups, she landed here. At Entertainment By The Fucking Minute.

"Noah is bigger than U2! Good evening, and welcome to the special weekend edition of Entertainment By The Minute. I'm Donna Wedbetter, and in our top story, Society Magazine today released their annual In/Out list, and in a shocking surprise, Noah is *in*, while the Irish rock band U2 is *out*." Donna stopped reading the TelePrompTer, because U2 had never been out, so surely there was a mistake. Right? She turned her head to the wings. "Can this

be right? U2's been in since 1983, how can they be out? I know he's Noah, but still –" She saw a crew member frantically gesturing to the area in front of her and remembered that her audience was the camera in front of her and turned to it. "Sorry about that. This is just shocking news. Absolutely shocking. Ace reporter Derek Deckenblacker is in the field, interviewing U2. Derek?"

Derek Deckenblacker appeared on the monitor, microphone in hand...clad in a Spongebob Squarepants onesie. "Donna."

"Uh, Derek," Donna said, "I thought you were going to Ireland to interview U2." That was where he was supposed to be. In Dublin. For Entertainment By The Motherfucking Minute.

"Oh, is that how it is?" Derek sneered. Such disdain coming from such a cute pair of pajamas elicited a guffaw from Donna, who tried to to hide it. "I interview U2, who are *out*, while you get to go after Noah, who is *in*? No way, sister. *I* get to interview Noah."

Donna took a deep breath and stared straight into the camera with whacked-out matriarchal disdain, as if Derek had just announced that he was dropping out of high school to pursue a career in the janitorial arts. "I thought you were a huge U2 fan, Derek."

The Spongebob pajamas and their occupant spoke, a petulant team of immaturity and youthful overconfidence. "Well, I was. Until yesterday. You saw the article – U2 is out! They're out! I only interview people who are in! Otherwise, there's no point in getting dressed in the morning. Or ever."

Donna sighed, wondered why she brought Derek along to this new job when she knew he was going to cost her this new job like she cost her her old job, and spoke to the crew member in the wings. "Can we get somebody else to go to Ireland to interview U2? And can I get some competent reporters? Please?" She put on her best fake smile, faced the camera again, and continued reading the TelePrompTer, with a whacked out suspicion that she and Derek were about to get fired. Again. "In other news, sunny weather grips most of our nation and a sudden dearth of attorneys has backlogged the court system -"

I n the pantheon of late-night talk shows - of which there were twenty-seven, approximately, because network executives know that a semi-successful formula was made to be copied ad infinitum, no matter the inevitable degradation of quality - three late-night talk shows stood head and shoulders above the rest:

"The This Night Show": A late-night talk show featuring all of the day's celebrity news.

"Talk!": A late-night talk show featuring all of the day's talk about all of the day's celebrity news.

And "Jimmy Alvin Live!" Jimmy Alvin was a former celebrity who had fallen off the day's celebrity news a lot of days ago due to his incessant ingestion of illegal narcotics and his perpetual passion for other people's pussy. At some point, as celebrities do, he went to a posh rehab facility in Beverly Hills for thirty days – where he ingested more narcotics and pussy than he did in a non-rehab facility month - and was declared 'cured' of his incessant and perpetual issues and was awarded a late-night talk show.

Which, to everybody's surprise, he prospered with, probably due to the ceaseless flow of drugs and women that came with his new gig.

So, as part of Steve's agreement to 'talk to the people' about the fact that they were all going to die, Jane booked him on "Jimmy Alvin Live!" "The This Night Show" and "Talk!" "Entertainment This Minute" and the twenty-three others were clamoring to book Steve, but Jane knew that Jimmy Alvin was the #1 show after the news and that he was a sucker for a good rehab story. Everybody deserves a second chance, right?

Steve sat backstage of the show in the green room in Studio City on a Tuesday afternoon, dressed in blue jeans, nice sneakers, and a dark blue polo shirt that Jane picked out for him, and watched the green room television as the opening credits appeared on the screen. He didn't really want to be here, but he did tell Jane he would do this, and maybe, just maybe, there was some good to come out of it. Steve was beginning to understand, a little bit, what Jane was saying about the human race. They were basically decent people, seemingly. Maybe a little dumb, but decent. It was hard to see why Chris wanted to kill most of them.

Jimmy Alvin appeared on the screen as Steve watched. "Thank you. Thank you. Welcome to the Jimmy Alvin show. I, of course, am Jimmy Alvin, every night, even tonight. Ya know, there's been a lot of talk today about who's in and who's out, because Society Magazine came out with their annual In/Out list, which we all look forward to, every year, of course. It's my favorite time of the year, except, of course, for that same time every year when Taylor Swift gets dumped by a boyfriend and writes a hit album about it." A rim shot set the audience cheering, and Jimmy continued. "Get this: in a shocking development, Society Magazine says that the Irish rock band U2 is 'out,' while Noah is 'in.' Well, shocking to some people. I mean, U2 has been in for a long time, and it's about time somebody came along to push them out. But, of course, the band isn't taking it too well. Over in Ireland, Bono says that today is 'Sunday Bloody Sunday.'" Another rim shot set the audience cheering, and Jimmy continued. "And what about this Noah guy, huh? I mean, really, he can beat U2, but can he beat our building permit system?" Another rim shot set the audience cheering, and Jimmy continued. "That system's a dinosaur, isn't it? In fact, it's such a dinosaur, Noah said he's going to take it and pair it with Betty White and put them both on his boat." Another rim shot, Steve got up out of his chair, and Jimmy continued. "But seriously, ladies and gentlemen, we have a real nice treat for you tonight. A real nice treat. Our first guest – and our only guest tonight, really, because he's that big – heck, even Society Magazine said he's big – is, without a doubt, the most famous guest that I, Jimmy Alvin, have ever had on the show. He's only been on the scene for a few months, but in that time he's captured international attention. He's building a ship out in the harbor, he collects animals by the pairs, his favorite color is ocean green, please give it up for Noah!"

Steve entered the stage from the wings, from behind a garish blue velvet curtain, walked onto the plastic-wood stage, and noticed that there were lights everywhere. On his face, on his body, on the stage, everywhere. *Everywhere.*

And people. Cameramen, producers, script supervisors.

And audience.

Everywhere.

The noise in the room grew to a gaudy level. As he walked towards Jimmy he looked out at the seated audience and they were no longer seated. They were on their feet.

Cheering.

For *him.*

He stopped walking. What the hell? Oh, crap, Steve thought to himself, if Chris heard him say that he'd be on kitchen duty for a week. He quickly corrected his thought to *what the heaven*?

The room volume was now blaring as Steve approached Jimmy

Alvin on the stage of "Jimmy Alvin Live." Television viewers would later note that that the hub-bub was not unlike the first time the Beatles played the Ed Sullivan Show.

Jimmy and Steve shook hands and a young woman in the third row fainted.

Jimmy directed Steve to a chair on stage and a woman in the first row gave birth. To a boy she named Noah, of course.

Steve sat in the chair on the stage and the entire seventh row screamed, swooned, and wanted to sex Steve. Even the men.

Jimmy sat down next to Steve. "Wow, Noah, the crowd really likes you."

"Yeah, I can see that," Steve said, his mind still reeling. And then it came back for a second. "Wait, I'm not Noah."

"What would you prefer to be called?"

"Well, my real name is Steven Easdale.," Steve replied. "Just call me Steve."

"Alright, we'll call you Steve."

At that moment the crowd started chanting; at first, a low rumble, then a louder rhythm, like somebody walking on a gravel path with combat boots.

No-ah. No-ah. No-ah.

Steve wanted them to stop calling him Noah, he really did, but his attention was elsewhere.

"That's quite a crowd you've got there, Mister Alvin."

"Yeah, well, that's the Cat Litter," Jimmy said. "That's their nickname. They're pretty boisterous, sort of like a cat in heat." The crowd stopped chanting No-ah and started making cat-in-heat noises. *Waaaaiiiiiiiiiiinnnnnnnnnaaaaoooowwwwwww!*

"Will you be taking any cats in heat on your boat, Noah?" Jimmy continued. "Uh, Steve? Sorry."

"That's okay," Steve said. "Uh, cats in heat. I don't know when the cats will be in heat. It depends on when we sail."

On the corner of the stage a butler stood.

Yes, a butler.

An older man, not much hair on his head, but what there was was white. Black pants, black vest, black bowtie, white shirt, white gloves, white hair.

Holding a silver tray with cocktails balanced upon it.

Again.

"Your drinks, sir."

The butler approached Steve and handed him a mimosa, his usual drink. Jimmy Alvin took a gin and tonic, his usual drink. The butler then wandered out into the seated audience, passing out their favorite alcoholic drinks to each member of the audience.

"Who's that guy?" Jimmy asked.

"I have no idea," Steve said, and it was true. It kept happening, and he thought maybe it was some perk of human celebrity. "He seems to follow me around. With drinks. I like him."

"He's got his own butler, ladies and gentlemen!" The crowd, who was now into their first free drink of the evening, screamed and cheered as if though their first free drink was a free car. The butler, whose tray was now empty, left, and Jimmy Alvin continued his interview with Steve. "So when do you expect to hang ten, so to speak? Set sail, so to speak?"

Steve took a sip of his mimosa. "You know, originally, we were supposed to leave last week, but delays and all that. Now it just depends on how long it takes to finish the boat. We've had to get reports and permits, and we've had several cost overruns, so we have to find some more money to pay for it all –"

The sound of a cash register drowned out the rest of Steve's reply and the crowd got even louder. Jimmy Alvin jumped up like he had been hit with an electrical charge.

"Money?" he yelled. "You said the magic word!"

"I did?" Steve asked. Magic word? What the heaven was going on?

"Yes! Whenever our first guest says 'money,' we have them give away five hundred dollars to one lucky member of our studio audience!"

The crowd was so loud now that they were even drowning out Steve's thoughts. He had never heard anything this loud, not even at Jimi Hendrix's celestial concerts, which were very, very loud. "You get to give it away to whomever you want!"

Wow, Steve thought, I am going to give money to people and make them very happy and – wait, wait. Orders. I have orders. Steve's mind teetered on the edge of something that he didn't like. Like being on a cliff above a canyon of snakes and being quite unsure of the cliff's stability.

He cleared his throat and refocused. "Mr. Alvin, that's not why I'm here. I'm here to talk to the people about the upcoming flotsam -"

"Flood?" Jimmy Alvin asked.

"Oh, yeah," Steve said, remembering the correct word. He figured he was getting better at this language thing, because he didn't even have to look that one up. "I'm here to talk to people about the upcoming flood."

"Here you go, Noah – Steve." Jimmy Alvin said, and handed Steve five hundred dollars in twenties. "Just take this cash up into our studio audience, and give it to somebody! Anybody you want! Anybody at all! Go!"

The cliff started to crack, but Steve didn't notice. He thought that maybe if he did this one thing for Jimmy Alvin he could do what he came here for. Couldn't hurt, right? "Can I talk to the people after that?"

The cliff started to give way and the snakes licked their lips. If snakes have lips.

"Sure," Jimmy Alvin replied, with a smile plastered on his face like a fresh advertisement on the side of a run-down building. "Talk all you want! You're Noah!"

The Cat Litter began to chant, quietly at first, crescendoing to a low roar. "No-ah! No-ah! No-ah!"

Steve took the money and headed up into the audience, who

were seated stadium-style, with each row a little higher than the next. He spotted an attractive blonde in the first row and went to her and handed her the money.

And then pulled it back.

And the crowd exploded with glee.

Steve handed the money to a well-dressed man in the third row.

And pulled it back.

And the crowd erupted with joy.

Making his way to the back row, Steve handed the money to a child, sitting next to his mother.

And pulled it back.

And the gathered throng rejoiced in an avalanche of pleasure.

Finally, Steve took the money and threw it up in the air over the audience, like a first world country air bombing a hungry third world country with rations.

"You made it rain," Jimmy Alvin said.

Steve, who by now was halfway down the cliff and showing no signs of saving himself (much like Wile E. Coyote in every Roadrunner cartoon ever made), was awash in adrenaline and mental filth. And could muster fewer words than ever.

"Wow," he said.

"Yeah, giving away money?" Jimmy Alvin replied. "It's something we do every night. People like money."

"They do," Steve said, his mind in some faraway land he kind of liked, but didn't at all recognize. "They do like money. And they like me."

"Yeah, Noah, they do," Jimmy Alvin replied. "They really like you. You're *in*."

In, Steve thought. I'm *in*. Hip. Cool like Johnny Cash. Interesting like Albert Einstein. Desirable like James Dean. Sexy like Elvis Presley. Looked up to like Chris....oh, shit.

"Look, Jimmy," he began, as the studio went silent and a spotlight shone on him from on high. "I want to talk about this whole boat thing. I mean, it's sort of the whole reason I'm here. And people need to realize that if they want to live -" At that moment the ground below the cliff opened up and Steve fell through, down, down.... "Wait, Jimmy, what if I do this?" Steve took his hands, palms side up, and pretended to raise the roof, and the crowd went nuts, as if Steve was the Beatles in 1967.

"Wow," Steve said, as his mind grew cloudy. "Look, Jimmy, I, uh, want to, uh, talk about humanity, uh - What if I do this?" Steve did something resembling the Macarena making love to the Electric Slide; it was the only dance he knew. Men in the crowd fainted. Women in the crowd had orgasms. And children in the crowd started writing memes that would appear on the Internet tomorrow.

"How does it feel to be 'in,' Noah?" Jimmy Alvin asked. Steve hit the floor of the canyon and realized *damn, I'm in.* After only being on this stupid planet for a couple of months! "Well, to be honest, Jimmy, it feels good. Real good." He moved his arms and his legs, repeating his dance.

Then he had another idea that he knew people would love.

"Can I sing a song, Mr. Alvin?"

"Sure, Noah. Do what you like," Jimmy Alvin said with a yawn.

THIS was his moment, Steve thought. His spotlight in the sun. HIS time to get up in front of an audience, to hold them in his hand, to have them hanging on every word, to sing words that he'd written, words that the audience takes and twists into meanings that he could have never intended, words that make them feel good.

He didn't have any words, he realized, but he sure could make some up. He had taken Robin Williams' Celestial Improv Class, he could make up words all day!

Jimmy Alvin moved to the side of the stage as the spotlight came back on and a microphone on a stand emerged from the center of the stage. Steve cleared his throat as the house band started playing a sweet big band riff, as if though Frank Sinatra were in the room.

"You like me," Steve began, sounding exactly like Frank Sinatra. To himself, anyway. Nobody else could hear him because the crowd was as loud as 72 jumbo jets taking off at the same time on the same runway.

"You like me," he continued, searching for words as his soul slipped into black muck and mire, "'cuz I am me, and I drink beef tea, up in heaaaaaaaaaaaven!" It was true; beef tea was a delicacy.

"You like me," he continued, "I don't need an inquiry, this I guarantee, let's open a delicatessssssssen!" The crowd grew louder still, as if they were all hungry for sliced meat sandwiches. And beef tea.

"You like me," he roared, "Kentucky coffee tree, advanced academic degree, war of the Spanish succession!" Steve wasn't sure what these words actually meant, but they rhymed. And the crowd was eating it up like it was actual sliced meat sandwiches. And beef tea.

"You like me, you like me, you like me, armegeddddddddon!" Steve threw his arms out to his side like a crucified hero...and the building shook from the roar of the crowd.

"That was great, Noah," Jimmy yelled over the crowd. "Don't you think so, studio audience?" At that moment, seismologists at UCLA saw their instruments go crazy and started alerting authorities that a 7.6 earthquake had struck Studio City, when in fact it was just Jimmy Alvin's studio audience.

"Alright! You're definitely a star, Noah!"

"I guess I am," Steve said, his mind a whirlwind of energy, fog, and a strange new darkness that he had never felt before. "A star. Yes, I am. I. AM. A. STAR! And it feels GOOD!" He paused as the ideas flowed. "You know what, Jimmy? I think I'm going to come out with my own, uh, music CD." The studio audience melted into a quivering mass of applause.

"And I'm going to change my name to an unpronounceable symbol." Hey, it worked for Prince, right?

The room went silent and the UCLA seismologists went back to their small talk and coffee.

"That's been tried, Noah. Without much success, I might add."

"Okay, then," Steve's mind raced. He had lost the audience, now he needed to get them back. It was like the time he saw Jimi Hendrix cover a Justin Beiber song; about halfway through he stopped and went into 'Foxy Lady.' It was brilliant.

"Okay, then, I'm going to change my name to...to...to T-Bone!" The audience blew up again and Steve silently thanked Jimi Hendrix for the inspiration. "And I'm going to come out with my own line of clothes! Yeah! T-Bone T-shirts!" He threw one fist in the air and the crowd followed suit, each person throwing one fist in the air.

"And I'll have my own website, and Twitter feed, and memes, and cats with cheeseburgers....and..."

"Now, Noah –" Jimmy Alvin began.

"T-Bone."

"T-Bone – right, hey, T-Bone, we have a friend of yours backstage. She wanted to come on our show and be a part of all of this. Ladies and gentlemen, say hello to Jane McKee, T-Bone's girlfriend!" The audience politely clapped as a woman with brown shoulder length hair, brown eyes, soft pink lips, and eyes that were trying to incinerate Steve walked onto the stage from the same wings that Steve had entered from earlier. Steve, in his bottom-of-the-canyon altered state, didn't recognize her.

"Steve?" the woman asked.

"I'm T-Bone, baby." Clearly the woman didn't know who she was talking to. T-Bone, uncrucified hero.

"Steve, I thought you were going to talk to them. Tell them how they can rearrange the future! What happened to you?"

What happened to me? Nothing happened to me, Steve said to himself. I'm still here. On TV. With Jimmy Alvin. And an enraptured studio audience.

"They like me, baby," Steve said. "Watch." Steve repeated his dance from before, his limbs flailing like a kite that was about to hit the ground. The crowd meowed as loud as before. "See? They like me. A lot."

The woman continued. "But Steve, I thought -" The woman pointed to the audience. "They're all going to drown. There'll be nobody left to like you, then. You need to talk to them!"

"Wow, Steve, she's a spitfire," Jimmy Alvin said. "Where'd you find her?"

"They like me, baby," Steve said to the woman. "Just like the people in the park, and the people at the grocery store, and the people at the -"

"But we had a deal, Steve. I'm going to teach you how to sing, and you're going to teach them how to live. That was our deal!"

Steve scoffed at what the woman was suggesting. "I *know* how to sing, baby. Listen." He cleared his throat, threw his hands up in the air as if about to deliver a James Brown Sunday Sermon, and again sang, "you like me, 'cuz I am me, and I drink beef tea, up in heaaaaaaaaaaven!" The gathered throng came within a centimeter of fainting – or that's what it felt like - and Steve stopped and spoke to the woman. "See? I know how to sing. I don't need you."

The woman looked at the audience and addressed them. "People, you have to listen! We're all going to die, unless we change! We need to start protecting our environment and respecting each other and –"

Jimmy Alvin walked over to the woman, put his finger on her lips to shush her, and turned to the audience. "You know, Steve, we have another tradition on this show. Whenever one of our guests gets a little, shall we say, 'preachy,' we bring out The Soapbox!"

The audience went bonkers again, and Jimmy Alvin went to

his side-stage desk and pulled a plywood box from underneath it. He turned it towards the audience and Steve saw that it had the word "Soapbox" written on it in large letters.

"Go ahead, sister, get up on there and tell it like it is," Jimmy said to the woman. She put one foot on the box, hesitated, and brought it back to the floor.

And spoke. "This is ridiculous. What happened to you, Steve?"

A faint chant from The Cat Litter; a chant that grew louder and faster each time it was repeated. "Go.......away........baby. Go....away....baby. GO...AWAY...BABY!"

Basking in the glory of unbridled adulation, a feeling that Steve couldn't even articulate much less find words for, he knew that everybody in the room had his back. Everybody in the room was his best friend. Everybody in the room would die for him.

Everybody but one person.

"They want you to go away, baby," he said to the woman. A tear slithered down the face of the woman, and for a moment Steve felt something...different. Something deeper than the glory of unbridled adulation. Something soft. And hard. At the same time. What the heaven?

"What do *you* want, Steve?" the woman asked. The Cat Litter purred and Steve's deep feeling disappeared faster than a Donald Trump campaign promise.

Steve fell further still down the collapsing cliff and landed in the snakes, who were waiting to devour him with their snake lips. "You better go away, baby."

"Security!" Jimmy Alvin yelled.

"But Steve, I loved you" Yeah, the woman loved him. Just like the audience loved him and Jimmy Alvin loved him and everybody on this planet loved him.

"It was just doggie love, baby."

"I think you mean puppy love, T-Bone," Jimmy Alvin said, and the audience laughed like their uncle had just told a dirty joke.

"It was just puppy love, baby."

"It was a misguided crush, you asshole," the woman quietly said as tears welled up in her eyes and she started sobbing.

A security guard entered from the wing and escorted the sobbing woman away.

"Well, that was awkward," Jimmy Alvin said, as the Cat Litter went quiet for the first time since the show began. "Yes," Steve replied. He looked out at the Cat Litter and wondered how he was going to get them back on his side.

"Just another groupie, right Noah?" Jimmy Alvin nudged him in the side with his elbow.

"Just another groupie, Jimmy Alvin. They all like me." An idea hit Steve, an idea that would propel him back to the heights of unbridled adulation. Or so he hoped.

"Can I sing another song, Jimmy?" he asked.

"Sure, T-Bone. You're the celebrity of the moment. You can do whatever you want!" The sound of anticipation enveloped the room like fog envelops a small town in a horror novel, and Steve began to sing.

"You like me, I don't need an inquiry, this I guarantee, let's open a delicatesssssssen!" A loud "MEOW" engulfed the stage as The Cat Litter voiced its appreciation, and Steve continued. "You like me, Kentucky coffee tree, advanced academic degree, war of the Spanish succession!"

Somehow, despite her seemingly incessant desire to ruin her own career, Donna Wedbetter kept finding newscasting jobs. Okay, so maybe the word 'news' is generous in that sentence. She kept finding jobs. On television. On lower and lower and lower rungs. It was like somebody had turned her ladder of success upside down, but she had managed to hold on anyway. She had bills to pay, right?

And she had started doing yoga three times a week. She found it really helped her state of mind; so much so that this new gig didn't bother her. It was just a job, right? Namaste, bitches.

"Good morning, shoppers!" she read from the TelePrompTer. "And a beautiful morning it is! I'm Donna Wedbetter, your Home Shopping Spree correspondent."

She had also started smoking weed four times a week. She was a fucking home shopping newscaster??!! Fuck! Namaste my ass! Pass the bong!

Still, she knew how to present a cheery face to the public. She

learned it back when she had a real fucking job, thank you very much.

"As you can see, I'm still in my pajamas, because, yes, this is the Saturday morning show on the Home Shopping Spree network. However, as you can see, these aren't just any pajamas, no." Donna pointed at the pajamas she was wearing, as bile rose up in her throat at the recognition of just how far she had fallen down the success ladder.

"These are our brand new," she continued, "just released this week, T-Bone pajamas! We're so excited here at the Home Shopping Spree, because these pajamas – well, see for yourself. They're just darling!" Darling, she thought. That's the word I'm using on television after ten years in the business. She swallowed hard.

"100% cotton flannel," she continued, pointing out the features of her pajamas, as instructed by the segment producer. "And here you can see two tigers and two lions and two lawyers, all headed towards the boat. We've got 5,000 pairs of each size of these jammies, and we're selling them right now for just three easy payments of $29.99! That's right, if you call now and ask for item #666, you too can be lounging around on your bed in your T-Bone pajamas. They even come in men's styles. With me, as always, is my trusty ace Home Shopping Spree cub reporter, Derek Deckenblacker. Derek?" She let the question of Derek's existence hang in the air, half expecting it to never be answered.

And then he walked out onto the stage. Donna had never actually seen him in person; he was as douchey in real life as he was on TV.

"That's right, Donna," Derek said. "I'm always with you. And I am your trusty Home Shopping Spree reporter."

And then he stopped.

"Don't you have something to say, Derek?" Donna asked, rubbing her temple with her right hand. This was going to be a long morning.

"Yeah," Derek continued. "Actually, Donna, I'm really sorry I got you fired from your last job at Entertainment By The Minute. I should have interviewed U2. I should have –"

Donna had some yoga - and weed - to get to, and this segment would be finished once it was finished (boy, that was deep!), so she wasn't really interested in listening to Derek blabber on with an apology or whatever. Because weed! The prospect of this afternoon's weed and yoga sesh greatly diminished her current whacked-out built-in matriarchal sense of responsibility for Derek Deckenblacker and his fuck-ups, so her level of interest in whatever he was saying was about negative five right now.

"Derek, bygones and all that. Can we get back to work? Or should I expect that we'll soon enough be working at the Pennysaver?"

"Penny saved is a penny earned is what my momma always said," Derek replied.

Donna sighed. "Why do I even try?" Derek walked off stage and she turned to the camera and read from the TelePrompTer. "Speaking of U2, ladies and gentlemen, we're proud to feature on next Saturday's Morning Shopping Spree the spectacular new benefit digital album, 'Batten Down The Hatches.' Recorded during one hectic session a week or so ago, it features U2 and all your other favorite artists, and all songs on the album are about T-Bone and his ship, and all proceeds will go towards the building of T-Bone's ship. I listened to a preview copy of the album last night, and let me tell you – it will be the biggest thing since the Beatles broke up. It's that good." Yeah, she had listened to it under the influence of yoga – and weed - but still, it sounded good. Or maybe that was the influence of the weed. Or the yoga. Namaste, bitches!

Derek walked back on stage. "Donna?"

"What now?"

"We're out of T-Bone jammies."

"Really?"

"Yep, we just sold out of them."

"Wow," Donna said, as Derek walked off stage.

"So," she continued reading from the TelePrompTer, "if you missed out on that deal, you're surely PO'd at yourself right now. Not to be confused with PJ'd. Ha. Ha."

She turned to the wings, where the segment producer stood drinking a cup of coffee. "Are these jokes supposed to be funny?" The segment producer gave her a thumbs up. "They are? Okay." She turned back to the camera. "Anyhow, ladies and gentlemen, you may have missed out on the T-Bone Jammies, and you may have missed out on the Charlie Sheen Winning kit a couple of weeks ago, and you may have missed out on the Eminem M & Ms that we had on our show a couple of months ago, but you're not going to want to miss out on this. No, this is going to be big. Bigger than all those things. Bigger than the Kim Kardashian home sex tape/build a family financial empire kit. Bigger than the Janet Jackson Tear-Away Lingerie Set. Much, much bigger. Ladies and gentlemen, item #667 on today's Home Shopping Spree is..."

She reached down below her desk and pulled up a bottle of perfume. "Eau D'T-Bone. That's right, here on The Spree, we've got the first fifty cases of Eau D'T-Bone, so if you want to be the first on your block to smell as 'In' as T-Bone, give us a call right now. Only four easy payments of $29.99. Let's smell it, shall we? Apparently," she read, not believing what she was reading and saying out loud, "this fragrance – for both men and women – contains actual sweat from the body of T-Bone. That's right, it smells like T-Bone. Let's smell it."

She opened the bottle of perfume, took a whiff, and threw up in her mouth a little bit. That's what happens to the human body when something smells like a cross between an unwashed jock strap and curdled milk. She swallowed her vomit and carried on, because she had bills to pay. And yoga and weed to get to. "My God! That *is* sweat!" She turned to the segment producer, who was calmly drinking his coffee, and asked, "Is it supposed to smell like this? It is? Okay." She turned back to the camera, tasted vomit again, and slowly carried on. "So...if you want to smell like T-Bone, just give us...a call. We've only got 1,000 bottles of this sweet...smelling...nectar, so give us a call, before it's too... late." She swallowed hard and wondered to herself if the taste of marijuana could mask this. And then Derek walked on stage.

"Donna?"

"WHAT?"

"We've sold out of the smelly stuff."

"God, people will buy anything, won't they?"

SCENE 6

Fame is a fickle mistress. One day you're on a famous talk show and everybody knows who you are and every company in the land wants to sign deals with you and all the women want to bed you and the next day you feel like you were run over by all of the Kardashian family on their way to a photo shoot.

So this is what an earth hangover feels like, Steve thought. It was almost exactly the opposite of a celestial hangover, which was a euphoric feeling of great joy and beauty. This? This sucked donkey balls. Steve knew it didn't, really, because a feeling can't suck anything, and what if the donkey was a girl donkey? But still, this was NOT a celestial hangover. By any means.

He staggered his way to the Ark Zone, where the Ark was located and where John was busy doing whatever John did. Steve wasn't even sure anymore.

"What up, dog?" he asked John, and then he tripped on something and fell to the ground, his face meeting terra firma beneath him like it was a rabid fan trying to get his autograph.

"You okay, Steve?" John asked.

"Yeah, dog, I'm fine," Steve replied through a quickly swelling lip.

"What are you talking about? I'm not a dog. And what's with the clothes?"

Steve rolled over, sat up, and looked at his clothes. Ah, yes, his clothes.

"You mean my threads? Check out my flava!" He gestured to his new silk shirt, which was completely unbuttoned and adorned with a laughing skull on its back. He gestured to his new $800 jeans, which rode down below his butt like Steve couldn't get them up over his hips. And he gestured to his new designer sunglasses, which were designed by somebody Steve had never heard of, but all the cool people were wearing them, so they didn't suck donkey balls. Girl or otherwise.

John rolled his eyes. "I mean your clothes. And those sunglasses. Are you trying to get on television or something?"

Steve pulled his sunglasses down so could look John in the eye. "I've already been on televissle."

"Tele-what?"

"Last night, baby. I was on televissle. The fans demanded it."

"The fans?"

"It was the shizzy, my nizzy."

"Ooookay," John replied, and his face turned quizzical. "Are you okay?"

What the hell, Steve wondered. *Am I okay? I'm better than okay!*

"What do you mean, home fry? I'm better than okay. I'm the bomb. My peeps say so."

"Bomb? Peeps?"

"For shizzle, Home Depot."

John pulled out his smart phone and looked at the map on it.

"Yep, we're on planet earth," he said. "You must have misplaced your Big Dic, because you're talking weird. I don't understand it."

"Of course not. You're whack." A rustling to Steve's right and the butler was there with drinks on a tray.

"Your Manhattan, Mister T-Bone," he said, handing Steve a Manhattan. He turned to John and handed him a glass containing white liquid. "Your milk, John."

"Milk?" John asked as he took the glass into his hand. "That is all, butler guy," Steve said to the butler and the butler left. Everybody listened to Steve, right? Hell yes they did. Because he was T-Bone, that's why. And he was Noah. And he was motherfucking Steve Easdale, bitches.

"What are you doing?" John asked, still holding his glass of milk. *What am I doing?* Steve wondered, and he took a sip of his Manhattan, which was, frankly, the best Manhattan he'd ever had. *What. Am. I. Doing?*

"Why, Johnny, I'm merely representin'," he replied.

"Representing what?"

"I'm living the life."

"The life of a what?"

Damn, Steve thought, John was very annoying all of a sudden.

"The life of a fly playa who has many many adoring fans. Let me point out that four of them spent the night at my crib last night. At the same time. Give me a pound, dog!" Steve put his fist up, looking for a pound from Annoying John, but Annoying John just kept talking. No wonder he was annoying. "Chris is going to kill you," Annoying John said. "This isn't why we're here. We're here to finish the boat, load it up, and set sail. And that's it. What happens to your adoring fans when you leave them behind? They drown. That's what happens to them. Then they can't get into your crib, or your bassinet, or even your Johnny Jump Up. What then?"

"Damn, John, don't be a playa hater!" At that moment, a sharp pain appeared in Steve's mouth, as if his tooth had been punched by Andre the Giant, and he grasped the bottom part of his chin with his hand. "Ow! My tooth hurts! Wow!"

"Are you okay?" John asked.

"Yeah, I – a little Manhattan might help." Steve took a sip of his Manhattan; the cold helped numb his tooth.

"Maybe you're just hungover."

Steve swallowed the Manhattan in his mouth and smiled at John.

"For shizzle."

"Listen, Steve, about our money problem," Annoying John said. Did this guy ever stop talking? "I was thinking -"

Steve cut him off. "I've got the solution for you, baby."

"I'm not your baby."

"Check this out, Broheim." Steve put his Manhattan down on the deck of the Ark and unrolled a rolled up canvas sign that he had tucked under his arm and stuck the sign on the side of the Ark. It said, in huge letters, "The Really Big Burger Company," and in smaller letters, "presents Noah's Ark."

"That's your solution?"

"Oh, it's just the start, Franklin D. Broosevelt. Check this out: once people see that the Really Big Burger peeps are on board, they'll be lining up to buy advertising on the Ark. We'll sell every square inch of this thing, for shizzle! And we'll be rich rich rich! With all kinds of bling bling! Give me a pound, dog!" Steve again held up his fist to Annoying John, who again ignored it. Steve ignored the ignoring and continued. "Look, home boy, we'll sell sponsorships for each of the animals – can't you see it? 'Cotton America Presents These Two Sheep?' And we'll sell forty sponsorships, one for each day! Then, every morning on the boat, we'll say, 'Day Twenty's activities brought to you by Handy Wipes, for those floods around your house.' Or at least that's what we'll tell them we'll say."

"What?"

"John, dog, we can't go on this trip," Steve said, as Andre The Giant punched his whole mouth. "Ow, what the hell?" "That's not our decision to make, Steve."

"I gotta stay here with my crew," Steve said through his clenched jaw. "They'd hate me if I went on the boat!"

"They wouldn't hate you. They'd be dead."

"You're so concrete, home improvement center," Steve said, feeling his jaw with his hand. He had never felt this much pain before, but maybe this is what it meant to be human. "Chill out. Where's my butler? I need another drink."

Steve heard footsteps nearby and the butler appeared, nattily dressed, with a tray of two drinks.

"Your Manhattan, Mister T-Bone," he said, handing Steve a glass filled with Manhattan colored liquid, ice, and a lime. "Your milk, John," he said, trying to hand John a clear glass filled with milk. John shook his head, ignored the offer, and turned back to the Ark, where he was trying to apply another fresh coat of gray paint to the hull. Except now there was a Really Big Burger sign in the way. "Thank you, butler guy," Steve said. "Can you bring me some of those peanut butter and banana sandwiches that you make? They're so good."

"I happen to have some fresh peanut butter and banana sandwiches on my plate, sir. Please, take a few." Steve looked down at the tray, which previously contained one glass of ignored milk and one glass of ignored milk only, and smiled. It was now piled high with fresh peanut butter and banana sandwiches.

"You're good, butler guy," Steve said "What am I paying you?"

"You're not, sir."

"Very good. "

"Not yet," the butler replied, and as fast as he had entered the Ark Zone, he left the Ark Zone.

John overheard the conversation, stopped trying to figure out where to continue painting the Ark, and turned to Steve. "This can't turn out well."

"Whatever do you mean, dog?" Steve asked as he took a drink
of his Manhattan. Damn if it wasn't the best Manhattan he had
ever had.

"All of a sudden, you don't want to go," John started. "You've
got your own butler, you're on TV, they're selling your sweat, you
talk funny – well, funnier than usual -"

Steve heard footsteps nearby again. John sighed as the volume
of the footsteps increased exponentially, like a freeway that had
just been re-opened.

"Hold that thought," Steve said. "The news posse is coming."
John sighed again. He seemed to be sighing a lot these days, Steve
thought. "The news posse?"

"For shizzy," Steve replied. It was a new word he had just picked
up while hanging out with his new friends. The English language
was weird, but so very cool. "My agent says I've got to keep my face
in the public eye so they don't forget about me. I am a star, after all.
So I've called a press conferizzle –"

"Your agent? A press conference?" John sighed again. "This
can't turn out well."

"It will. Watch while I do my thing, little G."

"I have work to do," John, said, and disappeared into the Ark.
Steve turned to face the oncoming throng of fans and tumbled to
the ground, his ankle twisting like a state fair pretzel. With a side
of cheese.

"Ow! What the hell is going on?"

A gaggle of reporters – at least, that's what Steve thought
they were called. A school of reporters? A flock? - entered, led
by a brunette reporter with short hair and an assertive face, an
assertive face that he recognized. She turned and spoke into the
camera that her camera man was carrying behind her.

"I'm Kyle Karpenter, Channel 3 news, here at the Noah press
conference, which is just about to begin." She turned and looked

at Steve, who cleared his throat and hobbled to the podium on his twisted ankle.

"Hello, members of the prizzle," he began. "Mad props to you for coming. And a shout out to all my homies for their support. I trust you all saw my appearance on the Jimmy Alvin show last night. Wasn't I great? Yes, I was. The greatest. Check the ratings. Best ratings ever. Now today, I'm here to not only grace your presence, of course, but to announce two things. First of all, I am opening a chain of restaurants. Yes, I am opening Planet Noah restaurants all over the world. We will be serving up two dishes from each type of animal. Get it? Two? Animal? Clever, isn't it? I thought of that myself. Use your Noah Gold Card and get a 2% discount. If we're out of something, we'll give you a raincheck. Get it? Raincheck? Another one of mine, of course. For shizzle. Secondly, I would also like to announce that, once the Ark behind me is completed, we will be running gambling cruises aboard it on Friday and Saturday evenings, weather permitting, just like the Indians, but with appropriate themes, of course. Two card poker, two thousand dollar stakes, a rain and jungle motif, with each blackjack table decorated in a different animal style. There will be a buffet, with all the trimmings, and a live band for dancing pleasure, and pit bosses dressed as me…it's going to be great. So great. The greatest. At this time, I will take any questions."

Annoying John appeared on the deck of the Ark behind Steve. "I have a question."

"Don't be frontin'!" Steve said. It was something he heard somewhere. "Talk to the hand!" He knew that hands don't have ears to listen, but was sure this meant something different. What did it mean? Did it matter? He was on top of the wizzle!

"Why are you doing this?" Annoying John asked.

Dang, Steve thought, Annoying John sure was annoying. Steve ignored his question and pointed to a man in the crowd who had his hand up. "Yessir, you – there."

"Yes, Mister Noah T-Bone, will you actually be on any of these gambling cruises?"

Ah, Steve thought, now that's a good question. "When my schedule allows, I will indeed make appearances on the cruises. A lottery will be held for a chance to get my autograph during my appearances, and autographs will be $100 a piece. $50 for kids 2 and under. $60 if you want me to put their name next to my autograph. It's a small price for such a famous autogrizzle. Next question?" He pointed to a woman in the crowd.

"Is there any truth to the rumor that you are also putting together a reality television show based on the Ark?"

"Well, now, people, come now," Steve said. "If we had a reality show based on the ark, we'd have to drown everybody else but the contestants, and then most of you'd be dead, right?" The gathered crowd laughed nervously, as if they'd just been told a very inappropriate, yet funny, joke. "And of course, we wouldn't want that, right? I mean, if all my peeps died, who would want my autograph?"

Another woman in the crowd spoke. "Noah, there is a rumor floating around the Internet that you and Taylor Swift were recently spotted shopping for forty pieces of lingerie for her, and that all of her ex-boyfriends were a little perturbed by this. Comment?"

"You know I can't comment on that," Steve said. "Let me just say that in due time Taylor and Angelina and Demi and Charlize and Cameron will all get their chance. So ladies, get in line -"

A loud noise rang out and a burning pain shot through Steve's chest, like he had been shot. He looked down at his 'Big Burger' shirt; yep, he'd been shot. He slumped to the ground and made crazy gargling noises. Not by choice, mind you.

The crowd went hush and a reporter from the crowd said, "Did you hear that? He said, 'blllaaaaaaaaaaaaaaaaaaaaaa–cccccccccccccccccctttttttttttttttttttttthhhhhhhhhhhh,' which clearly means, 'Beyonce is leaving Jay Z for me!'"

"I gotta call my newsroom!" another reporter said.

"I gotta call my bookie!" another reporter said.

Kyle Carpenter turned to her camera man. "Kyle Carpenter, channel 3 news – our top story tonight: Beyonce is leaving Jay Z for Noah! Or T-Bone. Or Steve. What's his name now?"

Blood pooled on the ground next to Steve and he blacked out.

SCENE 7

A hero's welcome greeted Steve as he returned to his celestial palace, his former home (a double-wide trailer) nowhere to be seen. Wine, women, and endless Prince concerts, complete with duets with Jimi, Otis, and Freddie Mercury, embraced the rest of his days as sweet young female celestial beings tended to his every beck and call. Apparently, he had finally done something right. Not one to argue, Steve embraced his newly gained royal lifestyle and never looked back...

"Is he going to be okay?"

A voice, familiar.

"I think so." Another voice, authoritative and unfamiliar. Fuck, Steve hated unfamiliar authority. "He didn't have any health insurance, so we're holding him here in this secure room until he can find a way to pay his bill, but –"

"No, I mean, physically, not fiscally." The familiar voice, female. Soft. Fluffy. Like a kitten or a pillow. Like a kitten pillow. Was there such a thing? "Is he going to live?"

Steve's mind lurched into gear, like a fifty-seven year old hot rod that had been garaged and undriven for thirty-four years. 'Is he going to live?' WHAT. THE. PHO? Ur, FUCK?

"Oh, sure, honey," the unfamiliar authoritative voice screeched. It wasn't really a screech, but Steve disliked unfamiliar authority so much that all voices associated with it were screeches in his head. "He was shot in his buttocks, but it was just a cheek wound. Cheek wound, buttocks? Get it? That's one of my own."

SHOT? Steve wondered who the voice was talking about. Surely it wasn't him; he was in his celestial palace, *being fed Nutella by Marilyn Monroe...*

"So he's going to be okay?" The familiar voice again.

"Oh sure. As long as he pays his bill. If not, he might have more than a cheek wound – he might find both of his legs broken by our hospital tough guy, Vinnie. Then he wouldn't be okay anymore." Steve listened to this bizarre conversation that was taking place as *Marilyn Monroe smeared Nutella on his left cheek and began to lick it off.* Who the hell was talking? "That's a joke, sweetie."

"Oh, uh, ha ha," the familiar voice replied. Softly. Sweetly. And then *Marilyn Monroe disappeared* and all Steve could see was black.

"How did he get so popular, anyway?"

"Haven't you heard?"

"Heard?"

"He's the new Noah." Wait a minute, Steve thought, *I'm* the new Noah. There's another one of me? Did they send somebody else down to finish the job that I started? And where is Marilyn? He looked around; all he could see was black. "You know, 'Noah built the Arky, Arky?'"

"Hmm. Never heard of him. We hospital people don't get out much. Always working or sleeping, you know. So he's a builder? A very popular builder? Kind of like Bob the Builder?"

"Yeah, you could say that, I suppose."

"Well, if he's as popular as the crowd outside seems to indicate, I think he should be able to find a way to pay his hospital bill. If he doesn't, it's curtains." She made the International Gesture For Throat Slitting with her finger. "Vinnie likes curtains. I gotta go on rounds. See if you can get some money out of him."

Steve heard a door close and realized he wasn't in his celestial palace; he was in a hospital bed.

On Earth.

Fuck.

"Steve." The familiar voice. It was Jane. Shit. "You bastard. You damn bastard. Where did you go wrong? I honestly thought you could help. I – you know, we humans don't really know what we're doing. We don't want to drown, but we don't know how not to drown. It all seems so inevitable now. We're going to drown, and even you can't save us. And you turned into a bastard, too. Which doesn't help. We like our heroes to be nice and friendly, like Superman or Underdog, not bastardly, like Bastardman, or – well, like you. Bastard. Dead bastard."

"Jane." To his surprise, Steve's mouth worked. Well, for one word. Good thing Jane's name was only one syllable. Steve heard rustling above him, like she was tossing a salad above his face.

"You're alive, bastard? I mean, Steve?"

"Sure," he replied, his eyes still closed. "I think. Is this heaven? Are you an angel?"

"If you weren't such a bastard I might be. But you'll never know now." Steve opened his eyes and there she was, her face inches from his, her smell enveloping him with comfort.

"Jeez, maybe I should have stayed unconscious," he said, rolling his eyes, "at least my unconscious wasn't calling me bastard all the time."

"Well, you sort of deserve it," she said, lightly punching him on his shoulder.

"Ow! Alright. I'll give you that. I am a bastard."

"Oh, Steve," she said, her eyes lighting up, her body suddenly atop his, fitting together like two puzzle pieces that don't belong anywhere else. "I've missed you. Sort of. "

Steve held her tight; at this moment he wanted to hold her tight for eternity. "I've missed you, too. Sort of."

Jane pulled her face away slightly and looked at Steve, a worry in her eyes. "Are you okay?"

"I think so," he replied, his body comfortable under hers like a worn-in couch in a fraternity house. "It was only a cheek wound."

"So I heard," she said, smiling. "Who shot you?"

"Well, nobody really knows, but they're apparently detaining 472 suspects at Guantanamo Bay," he replied with a smile.

"That's a lot of suspects for one cheek wound," Jane said, stifling a giggle. She lay her body back down atop Steve and he knew where he wanted to spend the rest of his life. There. Underneath this sweet human. After a quiet moment when neither one of them said anything, she pulled her face up and asked him, "so, when are you getting out of here?"

"As soon as I pay my bill," Steve replied. He didn't have any money, but he knew they had a bill for him, and he knew he had to pay it before they'd let him go. So he'd figure something out. Maybe he could be a doctor for a few days? Sure, he didn't know anything about doctoring, but how hard could it be? Throw on some scrubs and act all smart and shit. Steve could do that, right?

"You know," Jane said, drawing on Steve's lower lip with her index finger, "everybody's talking about the shooting. Well, actually, they were talking about you and Beyonce, but then Beyonce and Bono were spotted nuzzling at an exclusive L.A. restaurant last night, so you and Beyonce are pretty much finished."

"I was never with Beyonce," he replied, and put the tip of her index finger in his mouth. She tasted like gas station pecan log roll. A delicacy where Steve came from.

"People always make stuff like that up. It sells papers. And perfume. And books. And action figures."

"Action figures?"

"There's now a Noah doll, modeled after you," Jane replied, as she drew circles on Steve's nose with her finger. "But it doesn't really look anything like you. It looks more like a Ken doll with curly hair. Made in China, of course. And it isn't anatomically correct. I hope it isn't, anyway. I mean, I've never actually seen your, uh, package, but I assume it's better that the action figure."

"Does it come with any accessories?" Celestial action figures always came with accessories, at least the ones Steve liked.

Jane giggled. "It comes with T-Bone jammies and a little Ark, and some animals. I bought one, because I thought you were dead and I thought it'd be a nice thing to stick pins into when the rain starts." She rolled off of Steve and laid next to him on the bed, and Steve immediately missed her body. Sure, her body crushed him slightly, but it was a crush by his crush, which by law alleviates the crush, so he could deal with the crush crush. "There's also an action figure of me."

"Yeah?"

"Yeah. It's called, 'Go Away Baby Ex-Girlfriend.' It comes with a little soap box. I guess that makes me a celebrity, too, in a way." She rolled off of the hospital bed and stood on the sterile hospital room floor next to the bed and cleared her throat. "Steve, what happened to you?"

Steve pointed to a short plywood box in the corner of the room, labeled "Soap."

"Do I have to?"

Steve nodded his head.

"Oh, alright. If it'll make you listen to me for once." Jane stood upon the box; it made her almost as tall as the ceiling in the room. "What happened to you? One minute, you're your own man, an individual, and you're going to save this misguided planet from self-destruction, the next minute, you're on Jimmy Alvin's show, passing out money, dating Beyonce! I mean, really! Beyonce? We're all going to die soon, and all you can do is date Beyonce? When the fate of the entire planet is in your hands?" Steve cleared his throat and looked up at her. "Look, Jane, I never dated Beyonce. Honestly. And I don't really know what happened. I got up there, under the lights, and all of a sudden, nothing else mattered, because there was this unimaginable rush coming from the power that was my celebrity. All of a sudden, I was cool. Everybody liked me. And it went to my head. And my hands. And my feet. And all over!"

"Steve, you're just a rat trapped in a very public maze. You're a place for people to turn their lurid gazes, so as to mask their own dysfunctional lives from themselves!"

"I make people feel better about themselves, though, right? That's good, right?" Steve thought that was good. That's all people wanted, right?

"It's not good, you idiot! When you've got people spending all their time chasing you around for an autograph instead of living their own lives, it's not good. We are a society of voyeurs, insatiable in our appetite for vicarious living, unable to make something out of our own pathetic lives that doesn't involve staring at the television for three hours a night or competing with an eight year old for an autograph from some eighteen year old kid whose only real claim to fame is his genetic size advantage and his ability to dribble an orange ball. To an eight year old, he's a hero, sure, but my God." She took a breath. "Remember those people in the park who wanted your autograph?"

"Yeah," Steve replied sheepishly. Jane called him an idiot. Earth was fucking confusing, he thought to himself. Fucking? Is that right? He pulled out his Big Dic; yep, 'fucking' could be used as an adjective. And a verb. See? Confusing. Sorry, fucking confusing.

"Shouldn't they have been out writing an opera or volunteering at a soup kitchen or being a big brother to a fatherless child instead of chasing you around?" Jane asked. "You, who aren't even the real Noah? What kind of hero are you?" She stepped down from the box and crossed her arms.

"Well, I can sing," Steve said, as Jane's crossed arms seemed to cross even harder. Damn, Steve thought, that was supposed to be funny.

A doctor entered the room carrying a tray full of medicine cups. Steve looked at him and realized it wasn't a doctor; it was the butler. Although this time he didn't have any drinks - he had medicine cups - and he was wearing blue hospital scrubs. With a name tag that said 'Doctor.'

Jane noticed the butler and the two of them glared at each other like they had stolen each other's boyfriend. Steve stayed out of the way of that; it was like knowing that a 100 mile per hour slapshot was coming your way.

The butler turned to Steve and handed him a paper cup full of purple pills. "Your medicine, T-Bone." He then turned to Jane and handed her a paper cup full of black pills. "Your medicine, Lady Jane." She glared at him.

"But you're not a doctor," she hissed, and ripped the 'Doctor' name tag from his scrubs. "In fact, who are you? And what are you giving us?" She looked at her labeled paper cup of black pills and her rage bubbled to the surface of her face. "Hey, this says these are 'sense of humor' pills. There's no such thing! And there's nothing funny about any of this! We're going to die! Who the hell are you?"

Steve gulped down his purple pills, which tasted a lot like the Gummy Humans that all the celestials snacked on, and spoke. "Thanks, Butler guy. That is all." The butler glared at Jane one last time, turned towards the door, and left the room.

"Jane, you know what?" Steve said. "You're right."

"Of course I'm right, you bastard!" she seethed. Damn, Steve thought, he was getting nowhere with being nice OR funny. "You could have been a real hero, Steve, if you had decided to talk to the people, but – wait, did you say I'm right?"

"Yeah," he replied, and looked at her face, which softened just enough for him to think about liking her again. Some women are pretty when they're angry, Steve knew, but Jane was not one of them. She could have easily been a witch in a Disney movie when she was angry. "You're right," He continued. "And I can still help."

"Can you?"

"I can."

"How?" Jane's arms were still folded, but loose. Like maybe her anger was waiting to see how Steve could help before it decided which direction it was going.

"I can use my celebrity to warn the people about the flood! I can tell them to put less ice in the sodas, and to put Stonehenge in the right place, and to put some clothes on Britney Spears, and –"

"You really don't get it, do you?" Shit, Steve thought, I'm wrong again. "Do you really think that those are the problems that brought you to this planet to kill us all?"

Steve wondered for a moment, and realized she was right. Those were not the problems that brought him here to kill them all. And he replied appropriately. "Well, not all of you. There are several of you who are actually going on the boat -"

Jane's arms crossed more-crossier still and her eyes became poison-tipped daggers that made Steve realize he was wrong again. And that Jane was going to preach again. "Look, Steve, if ice in the sodas were the biggest problem facing mankind -" Steve pointed to the box in the corner of the room and Jane sighed and stepped up on it. "If ice in the sodas were the biggest problem facing mankind we'd be doing pretty well. It's not about that. I can guarantee you that the reasons you are here involve the destruction of the planet, endangered animal species, intolerance of other humans, intolerance of different religions, greed, corruption –"

"Jane, I know," Steve said. This was all in the study notes for a celestial class he took that he mostly slept through. But there was an exam, and Steve did read the notes for the exam. He looked up at her, her blonde hair nearly scraping the ceiling of the hospital room, her face a mixture of utter contempt and innocent beauty, and realized that no matter how wrong he continued to be, they were really on the same team. "I want to help."

"I don't know. I don't know if I believe you anymore. You're probably lying so that I'll bust you out of here. You're probably a bastard. My father would have called you a bastard. Among other things." She stepped off of the soapbox and refolded her arms. Battle arms, Steve decided to call them.

Battle arms or not, same team.

"Just give me a chance," he said, and formed his eyes into puppy dog eyes. At least that's how it felt. He hoped he hadn't made a mistake and formed them into bear eyes; bear eyes wouldn't get the desired result. In fact, bear eyes might lead to screaming and running, both activities that Steve wasn't interested in at the moment.

"It's too late," she said, her battle arms taking positions, like they wanted to outflank Steve. "Do you hear the crowd outside? They don't sound like they want any help."

"Sure, I hear them. But they're just a crowd of people. They can be swayed."

"I don't know," she said, her battle arms digging in like it was World War III in this hospital room.

"Come on," Steve said. "All I gotta do is yell, 'Beyonce' to them, and they'll all stop and listen and pay attention to me."

"Sure, they'll pay attention to you. But there's a good chance they're just going to want your autograph."

"They'll listen to me. I have a plan," Steve said, and realized he didn't have a plan. But he said he did. But he really didn't. He cursed his mouth, which often times said things his brain hadn't even considered.

"What's your plan?" Jane asked, and Steve knew he was going to have to make something up and leaned on his celestial improv training to come up with the best plan ever. "Well, I'm going to talk to them." There, that should take care of it.

"And?" Jane asked. Steve's eyelids lowered to half mast. Crap. He hadn't expected to be asked to provide this level of detail so soon. His plan was preliminary! And short! Talk to them! That's all he had!

And then Steve remembered the first tenant of improv: 'Yes And.' And he knew he had to create a plan to get people to listen to him using Yes And. And more importantly, he knew he *could* create a plan to get people to listen to him using Yes And. "I'm going to tell them," Steve said from his bed, and Jane pointed at the soapbox. He got up from his bed and stood on the soapbox, scraping his hair on the acoustic tiles that created the ceiling. "I'm going to tell them that they can save the planet and stop this nonsense by living right – by respecting each other and the environment and by getting to know their neighbors and by proving to my co-workers that, dammit, humans are good at heart and have the best of intentions. Yes, and I'm going to tell them that dropping donuts on people's feet is no reason for lawsuits and that catching colds in museums is no reason for lawsuits and that animals should be treated humanely and that religious differences are surface differences, that people are all the same underneath, and that guns are not an acceptable response to arguments and that reality stars should not be elected to office and that -"

"Stop," Jane yelled. "Wow. That really is annoying, isn't it?"

"Yeah," Steve replied. "It really is." He stepped down from the soapbox, displacing one of the acoustic ceiling tiles with his head.

"I'm sorry," Jane said. "I had no idea. I guess I really could use a sense of humor." She reached over the table, picked up her Sense Of Humor pills, and downed all of them. "Pay your bill and let's get out of here."

"How much is my bill?"

"I'll ask," Jane said, and the nurse appeared. "How much is his bill?"

"Well," the nurse began. "Let's see, there was that cheek wound. Then there was the security detail for you, and you ate four of the cafeteria meals, and you had one visitor, and a displaced ceiling tile -" she pointed to the ceiling - "so I figure that your bill for this hospital stay comes to just over $40,000."

"What?" Jane asked.

"Let me repeat. $40,000. It's too bad you don't have an HMO. Then it'd be $4.00."

"An HMO?" Steve asked.

"That's doctor talk," Jane said. "It's insurance. Nobody can really explain how it works, but it saves you money."

The nurse pointed at Jane with her pen. "She's a smart one, young man. I'd hang on to her. If you don't hang on to her, Vinnie's looking for somebody to hang on to. I gotta go do rounds." The nurse put the pen in her mouth and left the room.

"I can't pay my bill," Steve said. "$40,000 is a lot of money, isn't it? And I'm broke and -"

"Then let's slip out the window," Jane said.

"Really?"

"Really. We have some work to do. And it'd be kind of funny to slip out the window, according to my newfound medically induced sense of humor."

"Okay. I may not move so well, with this cheek wound and all."

"I'll help you." Jane helped Steve up to the windowsill of the open window and out onto the grass outside. She grabbed the soapbox and threw it out thewindow behind Steve and followed herself. From outside the window Steve heard the nurse re-enter the room. "I'm here to salve your wound – hey, where did you go? Vinnie! I need you to kick somebody's ass! The patient in room 666 left without paying his bill!"

INTERLUDE 5

After the Home Shopping Spree fired her for disparaging 'Eau D'T-Bone' live on air, Donna Wedbetter fell even further in her quest to retain some sort of journalism career. That's right, she went to work for MTV.

"Welcome to MTV news, I'm Donna Wedbetter," she said to the camera, her brain hungover from last night's marathon weed/orgy sesh. At least, that's what her guru called it - a sesh. And there was weed and sex with multiple strangers and gurus, so in Donna's head it was a 'marathon weed/orgy sesh.' "Our top story tonight is more of a question than a story, really. Who shot T-Bone? That is the question at the top of everybody's mind today. For more on this story, hopefully, we go to our own Derek Deckenblacker." She plastered a fake non-hungover smile on her face - it was something she was good at, perhaps the only thing, outside of sexually pleasing multiple strangers and gurus - and watched the screen. And watched. And watched. "Derek?"

A visage appeared on the screen; ah, yes, her young sidekick.

Can somebody be a sidekick if the whole purpose of their life is to fuck up yours? Wouldn't that make your sidekick your foe? Your rival? Your mortal enemy? Your fuckstick? No, that was last night.

"Yes?" he replied, his face that of a young lumberjack, with a beard and sideburns and a hilarious semi-mullety haircut. Business in the front, whatthefuck in the back.

Donna giggled. "Do you, uh, have more on this story, Derek?"

"Which story is that, Donna?"

"The 'who shot T-Bone' story?"

Derek's lumberjack visage turned serious. Finally, Donna thought, a serious face – maybe he wasn't a lost cause.

"Somebody shot T-Bone?"

"Didn't you hear?" she asked.

His eyes lit up like he had spotted giant redwoods in the distance. "Well, then, I gotta get home!"

"Derek?"

"Yeah, Donna?"

"Why do you need to go home?" Maybe he needed to get his ax to decapitate some redwoods, she thought. And giggled to herself again. She was going to need some more of that weed they had at the orgy last night and she was going to need it soon. It made her happy.

"Well, if somebody shot my dog, I should really be there to help him out, don't you think?"

"You have a dog named T-Bone?"

"I did, until somebody shot him."

Yep, he was still a lost cause, she realized. "Jesus Christ," she whispered. "I quit," much more loudly.

SCENE 8

Balboa Park on this Sunday was its usual early-fall self, if San Diego even has seasons. Early fall in San Diego means that the temperature has cooled off to 73 degrees Fahrenheit from its scorching summer high of 74 degrees Fahrenheit. And don't even consider the horrible winters when it's all of 72 degrees Fahrenheit!

But Balboa Park on this Sunday was its usual 73 degree self; families picnicking, people attending the latest museum exhibits, kite-flyers in the meadow. A general glaze of happiness drenched the place; malaise was not something Balboa Park was familiar with.

Nor was it familiar with protests. Or gatherings. This wasn't San Francisco, where hippies in Golden Gate Park were as common as fog in the Bay; no, this was San Diego, where sunshine and happiness kept people so far on the bright side of life that there was no reason to gather and proclaim publicly.

Until today.

Away from the carousel and museums, a podium with a microphone was perched in a clearing atop perfectly manicured green grass. Three rows of folding chairs were placed in a semi-circle so that the podium could be viewed from all of the chairs. And all of the chairs were full of people.

A woman, mid-thirties, dressed like she was homeless, was speaking. "Ladies and Gentlemen, I am here to announce that I, Mary, am pregnant with Noah's child. That's right, ladies and gentlemen, I am having your new ...uh, what's that word...messy eye...mess hall? Whatever it is, I am pregnant with it. Now, although Noah and I have never actually had sex, nor have we ever actually met, I am still pregnant with his child. Let's see, that would make the baby, uh, immacubate? Interactive? Yes, it's the interactive convection!"

A man, late-twenties, with shoulder length brown hair, dressed in flowing brown robes, shoved her off of the podium and onto the perfectly manicured green grass next to the podium.

"Ladies and Gentlemen," he began, "ignore this gold digger. For I am here. Yes, it is me, Noah. I have come to your planet, sent by your God, to warn you of impending disaster! The previous Noah, who also goes by the name Steve and T-Bone, was a fake. A hoax. A master impersonator, to be sure. He sounded convincing, certainly, but let me assure you, Ladies and Gentlemen, that I am the real Noah. I am him. He is me. Within my Noahness, I am here to save you, and your planet, from what is sure to be a nightmare of epic proportions. Now, in order to save yourself from this impending disaster, we must first do a few things. First of all, all the young ladies in the room must stand up. It's a decree from heaven."

He pointed towards the sky, and then towards the audience. "Stand up and let me see you. Stand up!" The women in the audience slowly stood up. "Now turn around, slowly." The women slowly turned around. "Alright, some of you can obviously go a long way towards saving this planet from destruction, especially you hotties in the third row -"

A man, late thirties, with a white beard and mustache, dressed in a flowy white robe, shoved the previous man off of the podium onto the perfectly manicured green grass.

"Ladies and Gentlemen, pay no attention to the man I just shoved out of the way, for he was not Noah. I should know, for I am Moses. *The* Moses. Yes, thank you."

Steve and Jane entered the clearing and took a seat in the last row. They had come to this event at Jane's request, to 'see what people were saying and to set the record straight,' according to her. But Steve had fallen a long way off the cliff and, thus, had a different idea.

"Now, here in the land of milk and honey, I'd like to do a little magic trick for you. A magic trick that only Moses can do. Please, ladies and gentlemen, stand up. All of you." The audience stood up. "Alright, now, I'm going to split you down the middle, right about here." He gestured to the split audience with his right hand. "And I'm going to ask this half of you to move to your right, and this half of you to move to your left." The audience moved as instructed. "I have parted the audience sea! Thank you! Try the veal and don't forget to tip your waitresses!"

A man, early 60s, with a pompadour, sideburns, and wearing a white jumpsuit festooned with tiny red and blue jewels, jumped up on the podium and shoved the man in the robes off stage onto the perfectly manicured green grass.

"Thank you, thank very much," he started, as Steve withdrew the loaded pistol from his pocket. It was time to end this false prophet nonsense. There could only be one.

"Wise men say," the man continued, "only fools rush in, but ladies and gentleman, the King is here. I am here to rock, I am here to roll. I am here in my blue suede shoes. I am here to be your teddy bear, with burning love, and I will save rock and roll, and I will save the planet earth, and I will save you. Now -"

Steve stood, lifted the pistol up, aimed it at the man at the podium, squeezed the trigger, and missed, because it was the first time he had ever shot a gun and he was generally not a coordinated individual anyway. The man screamed and ran off of the podium and away from Steve.

"Steve!" Jane screamed and looked at him, her eyes boring holes in his head like she was drilling to China.

"Don't you see what's going on here?" Steve asked. "That wasn't the King, that was an impostor."

Another man, dressed exactly like Steve, stepped up to the podium. "I am the real Noah!"

Steve raised the pistol, aimed it at the fake Noah, and squeezed the trigger again, hitting a tree three feet wide and three feet above the man. He really should have practiced shooting a gun before this.

"Steve! What are you doing?"

Steve put the gun down by his side and turned to Jane, her face a forest fire of anger and betrayal. "These people are all impostors!"

"It doesn't mean you had to try to shoot them! Where did you get a gun?"

"From butler guy. Aren't guns how you people solve problems down here? That's what my homies tell me! 'Got a problem? Put a cap in his ass.' I'm just solving a problem like a human would."

"But it shouldn't be that way. That's a fairly recent development!" Steve pointed to a plywood box a few feet away from the podium with the word 'soap' on it, and Jane reluctantly stepped up on it and kept going. "We would have gun control, because humans have proven time and time again that we can't handle the responsibilities that come with guns, but some people take the Constitution and its amendments too literally. And now you, trying to freaking shoot people!"

"There can only be one Noah," Steve replied.

"Who? You?" The tone in her voice suggested she didn't believe him. No, actually, it implied that she didn't believe him. No, okay, it came right out and concretely said that she didn't believe him.

"That's me, baby," Steve replied, doing his best to meet immovable object with great force.

"Don't baby me, you bastard! You're not Noah. You're Steve Easdale, hack singer, and you're a geek who likes gospel songs as sung by The King and peanut butter and banana sandwiches. You're not a deity!"

Steve looked out at the gathered crowd, who hadn't moved a muscle despite the threat of gun violence, and walked up to the podium and stepped up on it.

"Ladies and Gentlemen," he began, and as the crowd noise rose up like a tidal wave, his voice got louder and louder. "THANK YOU. YOU'RE TOO KIND. I REALIZE THAT YOU HAVE BEEN HOEDOWNED BY MANY IMPOSTORS -"

"Hoodwinked," a voice from the crowd yelled.

"YES, THANK YOU, I REALIZED YOU HAVE BEEN HOODWINKED BY MANY IMPOSTORS, BUT I'VE TAKEN CARE OF THAT, AND LET ME ASSURE YOU – YOU CAN DEPEND ON THE REAL NOAH. ME. I'M THE REAL NOAH. AND WE ARE STILL SELLING AD SPACE AND WEEKEND CRUISES ON THE NEW ARK -"

"STEVE!" As Jane yelled, the crowd went silent and Steve looked to his far left and saw two policemen at the back of the crowd with their guns drawn. He looked to his near left and saw Jane.

"Look, baby," he said to her, "you helped me out of the hospital, and that was great. And you taught me a few things along the way." Steve winked at the audience, who responded with a "whoooooooo" that indicated that that they knew that yes, he was talking about sex. "But here, baby, I'm king of the world."

The audience began chanting. "No-ah, No-ah, No-ah..."

Steve felt his face flush and this time he didn't check it. He knew it was flush, because he knew that this was his moment. His time to shine. His raisin dead entry.

He pulled out his phone and checked his Big Dic.

His raison d'etre.

This was why he was here.

"I am Noah, baby," he continued, "and I am king of the world. Kizzle of the wizzle. Cream of the crop! The sour cream on your taco! Don't you hear them? I mean, don't you feel it? The power? The rush? The feeling of invincibility? Of crazy power?" Steve began cackling wildly, like he was witch over a cauldron and somebody has just located the final ingredient for the spell, which, incidentally, was eye of newt. "There is nothing that can stop me now! This is my time to absolutely shine like the power that I am! I AM KING OF THE WORLD! I AM BIGGER THAN JESUS CHRIST!"

Generations later, the once-in-a-lifetime silence that enveloped Balboa Park at that moment would be discussed in history classes, alongside world wars and natural disasters. You could have heard a pin drop. Or a pie. Or a fluffy pillow.

"Wait," the first policeman, who had positioned himself close to Steve, said finally. "Did you say *bigger* than Jesus Christ?"

"Bigger than Jesus Christ?" the man who claimed to be Moses asked from the ground.

"Well, aren't I?" Steve asked. Well, wasn't he? Jesus wasn't here and if he was here, he'd never procure this kind of adulation. This reverence was reserved for Kardashians, Beyonces, and now him. Steve Easdale.

"Wow," the woman who claimed to be Mary said from the ground. "What a jerk. I really liked you Noah, too. But, you know what? I'm not really pregnant with your child. In fact, it was my boyfriend Vinnie who knocked me up. And that was no interactive convention, let me tell you. I was there."

The second policeman pulled out his radio and talked into

it. "We're going to need some backup. We've got a nutcase on our hands who thinks he's bigger than Jesus Christ."

Steve wondered what the hell was going on. It was true, after all. Couldn't these people see it? Why did this feel like dating again?

The first policeman reminded the second policeman that "he shot a couple of people, too – don't forget."

The second policeman spoke into his radio again. "Oh, right, I forgot, we got a couple of bodies, too."

"They're not dead."

"We got a couple of warm bodies, then."

Steve noticed a deafening silence had engulfed the area. "Wait, how come nobody's chanting anymore?"

"Dude," the first policeman said to Steve, "bigger than Jesus Christ? Really?"

"Well, yeah," Steve replied. "I mean, I'm here, now, and he's not here, and I've got peeps, and I'm the shizzy, my nizzy, fo dizzy, balizzy, skizziiiiiiiii –" What the hell was wrong with him?

"Dude," the second policeman said. "You're a nutcase, who thinks he's bigger than Jesus Christ." Both policemen held their bellies and laughed for what seemed like hours.

Finally the first policeman said, "that's hilarious. Now put down the gun and let's go."

INTERLUDE 6

After she was fired from MTV, or "quit," as she liked to claim, Donna Wedbetter took some time off to partake in weed-fueled orgies and to reassess her life choices. She changed her phone number so Derek couldn't find her, she blocked him from social media, and for once in recent memory, she actually felt good about what she was doing. Multiple orgasms and bong hits on a regular basis can do that to a person.

And then one day Court TV called.

"Good evening, ladies and gentlemen," she said, completely sober. She took a couple of days off from her weed and sex fueled evenings before starting this job because, well, maybe without Derek around she could make something last. Maybe. "Welcome to "Celebrity Docket," here on Court TV. I'm Donna Wedbetter, your Celebrity Docket correspondent. Ha! That rhymes. Sort of. Tonight, of course, we're talking about what everybody else is talking about. Yep, the arrest of Noah. For tremendous ego. Apparently, Noah thinks he's bigger than Jesus Christ."

She looked to the wings of the news studio. "Is that true? It is? Wow, that's unbelievable. What a jerk." She turned back to the camera. "Deportation proceedings are underway for Noah, who, we understand, doesn't have a green card, so if he is found innocent of the charges against him, he'll be sent back to where he came from anyway. Oh, and it says here he shot a couple of people, too. But still – bigger than Jesus Christ? Absolutely amazing. Let's go to our correspondent in the field, Derek Deckenblacker." Oh, fuck.

She turned to the wings of the studio again. "Derek? Deckenblacker?" The tech hiding behind the curtain nodded his head. Oh, fuck.

"Derek?"

"Yes, Donna?" Derek said on the screen, his stupid lumberjack hair and his jackass flannel shirt and his stupid motherfucking toothy ass grin….. "Donna?"

"Yes, uh," she started. "Do you have a report from the field?"

"Yes, Donna," replied, and stared at her through the video monitor.

And stared.

And stared.

And inside Donna something caught fire, a fire that had smoldered for a long time, a fire that had its origins in a long ago place, back at KDOG, when she still had a future and a life and possibility…until Derek came along.

"Can we hear it, maybe? Just maybe? Pretty please?" she asked, her voice rising, her anger boiling over like she was Krakatoa. "I mean, for once, Derek, can you do something without asking? Can you please just do something without me having to kick your ass?"

"Yes, Donna," he replied.

And stared.

And stared.

"Well?"

"Well, what?"

"Your report from the field?"

His eyes lit up and he collected himself, as best as Derek Deckenblacker could ever collect himself, which is to say not very well, and spoke.

"Oh, right. Well, I'm standing in this field, as you can see, and there are a few weeds, and some milk cartons, and what appears to be an old refrigerator with the door still attached – don't people know that that's dangerous?"

"Derek?"

"Yes, Donna?"

"Aren't you supposed to be covering the Noah trial?"

"Well, they told me to go out to the field, so that's where I am. At the field. Where my Aunt Mable used to throw ice-balls at us. It's the best field I know. So here I am."

Donna's mind, eroded from every job she'd ever had ruined by Derek Deckenblacker, blew up like a geyser, and she reached into her purse beside her, pulled out the pistol she had been carrying for self defense, and aimed it at the techie in the wing.

"Alright! That does it! The biggest trial in our lifetime is going on and you morons sent a bigger moron to cover it? God, what does a person have to do to get some decent help around here?" She squeezed the trigger and the techie fell.

"Does that help? Does it?" She squeezed the trigger again and whoever had come to help the techie fell.

"That?" She aimed the pistol at the camera men and the producer and squeezed the trigger three times, taking them all down. Her instructor at the gun range had said she was a good student and she smiled.

"There, now you all have to be replaced, and maybe we can get some decent help around here."

She put on her best newscaster smile and turned to the active camera. "That actually felt pretty good. In fact, it felt very good. I feel fine now."

"Uh, Donna?" Derek was on screen looking confused. Which is to say he looked the same as he always did.

"Yes, Derek?"

"Is everything okay?"

"Yes, Derek, everything's just fine. Hunky dory, even," Donna said, stroking the pistol that was now in her lap.

"I found a stink bug in the field."

"Derek?"

"Yes, Donna?"

"Can you come back to the studio quickly?"

"Sure, Donna. What's up?"

"Oh, nothing. I have something – uh, somebody I want to introduce you to." She sat back in her chair, silently stroked her pistol, and waited for the sirens.

SCENE 9: AND, IN THE END...

Today. Monday.

San Diego Superior Court is normally a pretty staid place; what goes on there is not always of much interest to the general public, unless more than three people died in any one event. The theorem that the courthouse employees have proven time and time again is that the sensationalism of any particular event is a direct function of how many people died in that event. Or how many celebrities were involved and might be showing up at the courthouse on any particular day.

But San Diego Superior Court had never seen anything like this.

Steve showed up at the court room on his bicycle, carrying a pizza box, wearing a fake mustache. He had grown quite weary of being recognized everywhere he went; people asking for his

autograph, wanting to have his baby, wondering how they could get on the boat. That's right, Steve had gone over the Celebrity Bump. Initially, celebrity is everything a person has ever wanted. Money, women (or men), adulation…but after a short amount of time, after realizing privacy has disappeared faster than a teenager at kitchen cleanup time, after you have questioned the true intentions of everyone around you – are they friends or are they vultures? - you've gone over the Celebrity Bump and you realize that celebrity isn't everything you ever wanted. And that you're just a very public rat in a very public cage.

And Steve didn't have any money anyway; he spent it all on the stupid Ark. And parties. Thus, the bicycle. And pizza box.

And it worked. He wormed his way through the huge crowd and shortly found himself inside the court house. He ditched the pizza box and mustache and entered the chambers, where his court-appointed attorney awaited. Seated in a chair just inside the door, the attorney was wearing a "Free Noah" t-shirt and looked oddly familiar. He stood to greet Steve.

"Hello, Noah. Jim Johnson." He smiled and the memory came flooding back to Steve. The cat. The stupid cat. "Remember?"

"You? You're defending me?"

"Yep. I am the last attorney on earth, so I am defending you."

"The last attorney? What happened to the rest of them?" Steve rubbed his forehead and rolled his eyes back in his head. He felt like he had a severe hangover – at least as it was described to him in his Big Dic - even though he didn't drink last night.

"Have you checked the list lately?"

"The list? The lizzle?" Ah, shit, Steve thought, I'm still talking like that. He pined for the days when not every word made him sound like an asshole.

"The list of people to be on the Ark?"

"Actually, no I haven't checked the list lately. I've been kind of busy. Uh, busizzle, I mean." Dammit. The fog wasn't lifting.

"Well, I have." Jim Johnson beamed like he had just scored a 1600 on his SAT.

"Yeah? How?"

"It's online. Like everything. And I am now on the list to be on the boat."

"What are you sizzling, uh, saying?"

"I am merely saying that it's fortuitous that every other attorney on the planet disappeared." His smile grew wider and took over the room, like it was vying to be one of the great Wonders of the World. "That's all. It's fortuitous."

"Um, yeah. For shizzle." Steve wondered how long his speech pattern was going to be so asshole-ish. He missed normal words, much like he missed normal life, where he could walk around heaven unnoticed and without pressure to perform and without the feeling of twenty pounds of fog surrounding his 2 pound brain. He rubbed his forehead again. "So how much is this going to cost me? I have no more money."

"LOL."

"LOL? What does that mean?"

"Look, Noah," Jim Johnson said, "money's no good where we're going anyway, so let me get you acquitted of the charges, and I won't charge you a fee, and we can set sail, so to speak. Hang ten, so to speak. Alright?"

The crowd outside was chanting. 'NO-AH! NO-AH!' Two security guards ran by to the burgeoning door of the courthouse and pulled it shut.

"Alright?" Jim repeated.

"Um, alright," Steve said, watching the security guards. This wasn't going to end well, he thought.

"That's what I'm talking about!" Jim continued. "Give me a pound, brother!" He held up his fist and Steve paused and then shook it with his hand like a handshake. "You and me are going to go a long way together."

"Jim, I've been thinking," Steve said, clarity finally arriving in his mind like a package that had been delivered to the wrong address but had now, after three months of back and forth between the delivery company and the sender, had finally found its purchaser. "I may have gone too far this time."

"Nonsense. We can take care of it. What'd you have for lunch today?"

"Peanut butter and banana sandwiches."

"You eat a lot of those, don't you?"

"Well, yeah. When I can find good ones." And he had found good ones, oh yes; there was a chain of Chez Noah restaurants that had sprung up all over Southern California and they delivered. And, because he had said they could use a picture of his face in their advertisements, all food was gratis for Steve. Which meant a shit-ton of Peanut Butter and Banana sandwiches. Fresh peanut butter and banana sandwiches, even!

"We'll use that."

"For what?"

"We're going to plead temporary insanity, because you ate too many peanut butter and banana sandwiches. Nobody would actually compare themselves to Jesus Christ, if they weren't temporarily insane, anyway. Seriously."

"Uh, yeah, seriously," Steve replied. He wasn't sure this whole idea was going to work, but all of a sudden the focus in his brain pivoted to the fact that he was hungry. Maybe somebody could run out to a Chez Noah and get him some sandwiches?

"We'll beat this."

"All rise for the honorable judge Noah," somebody said.

Everybody in the courtroom rose and an old man wearing a black robe shuffled in. In his left hand he held a jar of peanut butter; in his right a spoon.

Wait, Steve thought, Judge Noah? He looked at the old man. Long gray hair, mustache, beard, drab brown robe...and on his right hand, a Grateful Dead bear tattoo.

And when he made a fist, the bear danced. And when the bear danced, he giggled. He was giggling right now, because the dancing bear was dancing, because the old man was making a fist. Duh.

"You?" Steve asked the judge.

"Who'd you expect?" Noah asked, as he looked up from his fist. "Judge Judy?"

"But you said you had Arachibutyrophobia."

"I made that up."

"To get out of this?" Steve asked.

"You catch on fast."

"You know the judge?" Jim asked Steve.

"He's no judge," Steve said.

"Shh!" Jim put his finger to his lips. "Don't say that about the judge! Don't you wanna skate?"

"I don't know how to skate."

"That's lawyer talk for 'go free.'"

A woman in business attire entered the courtroom, carrying a briefcase. She went to the bench adjacent to Steve and he recognized her instantly.

"Julie?"

"Steve," Julie Boboolie replied, her face a blank canvas.

"What are you doing here?"

"I'm the prosecuting attorney."

"Whoa."

"You know the prosecuting attorney, too?" Jim asked.

"That's no prosecuting attorney," Steve said, wondering in his head exactly what the hell was going on.

"You sure know how to win friends and influence people, don't you?" Jim said. "You gotta say nice things about the opposition! Wait – that can't be an attorney. I killed them all." He looked up with a quizzical look on his face, like a kid who just heard that babies don't actually come from storks.

Judge Noah banged his gavel on the podium and spoke. "I now call this court room to order. People versus Steven Easdale, docket number blahblahblah…" He looked right at Steve. "Look, kid, let's spare the legal nonsense. You need to finish the Assimilate and Accomplish mission. You've assimilated, but you haven't accomplished crap. And this is your last chance."

Julie turned to him. "We've been warning you, Steve. Who do you think made you fall down? And who do you think shot you?"

"You shot me?" All of a sudden, clarity kicked Steve's mind in the nuts and he understood several things.

"Well, not me, per se, but one of our, ahem, minions."

"The Moral Majority?"

"The Moron Majority," Julie replied with an eyeroll.

"The Religious Right?"

"More wrong than right."

"Focus on the Family?" Steve asked. At this point he was just cracking jokes because, frankly, he was nervous. And he didn't like serious things. But mostly he was nervous. This situation was going somewhere, and although he didn't know where, he did know he wasn't sure he liked it.

"Riiiiight. Look, Bill Fofill shot you, because he was getting annoying and needed to shoot something, but it's not important, kid. What's important here is that this is your last chance. We're tired of waiting around. If you don't finish the Assimilate and Accomplish mission in the next week, they're going to ask Noah to do it. I was hoping they'd ask me to do it, but no." Julie sighed. "'Watching Reruns of Gilligan's Island and Promising That Your Tour Will Be Less Than Three Hours doesn't make you qualified to drive a boat' or some such crap."

"Why didn't Noah just do it in the first place?" That would make sense, Steve thought. Noah knew what he was doing; Steve surely didn't.

"Young man," Noah spoke from the bench, "that never works.

The sequel is never as good as the original. Look at Michael Jordan's comeback or the movie 'Grease 2.' If I had tried to do it again, production values would have been down, the script would have weak, and nobody would ever remember Noah 2.0. Plus it would have diminished the first time, which, I must say, was damn near perfect. That's why I didn't come back to do it again. Plus, I might have developed hodophobia.

"Homophobia?" Steve asked.

"Hodophobia, dumbass," Noah replied. "Fear of travel."

A female brunette reporter with short hair and an assertive face burst through the double doors at the back of the court room, a cameraman in tow.

"Wow, this is quite a scene," she said, surveying the court room. She made a 'roll it' motion with her fingers and turned to the camera, which now had a lit-up red light on top of it. "Good evening, viewing audience. I'm Kyle Karpenter, Channel 3 News, and I am here, inside the courtroom, at the trial of the century, where Noah is being brought up on charges of tremendous ego. Oh, and, uh." She pulled a notebook out of her pocket with her free hand, rifled through it, read some words, and continued. "Attempted murder."

Judge Noah banged his gavel. "He's not Noah."

"That's what everybody says," Kyle Karpenter replied, as she turned back to the camera and winked.

"No, really, he's not," Noah said. The court room was silent for a split second, and Noah continued. "I am."

"The last time somebody said that, he got shot," Kyle replied. "By this man. Allegedly. So be careful."

Noah banged his gavel seven times and leaned over to look at Kyle, like he wanted to make a point. "Look, young lady – hey, do you want some peanut butter?"

"That's a weird question," Kyle said, and then shrugged her shoulders. "Sure."

Noah sat back down on the judge's bench and produced

a spoonful of peanut butter for Kyle, who placed in her mouth deliberately and slowly. "Wow – that's the best peanut butter I've ever tasted. It's almost – it's almost heavenly."

"Of course it is. Look, young lady, I am Noah. How can I prove it to you?

"Well, let's see, do you know the whole song?"

"Of course I do."

"Can you sing it?"

"Of course I can." Noah, who hadn't been asked to sing by a woman in about 746 years, found some fountain of youth shit inside of him - having a beautiful woman ask you to sing can do that to a guy, even a 2,057 year old guy - and sang the entire 'Arky Arky' song like he was Marvin Gaye. Sexy, sultry, yet caring, all at the same time. He didn't tell Kyle that he had taken singing lessons from Marvin Gaye himself, because a man shouldn't reveal his teachers when it came to love, right?

Another woman, early twenties, wearing a 'Free Noah' t-shirt, burst through the doors at the back of the courtroom.

"I'm inside! I'm inside! Yeah! Dude!" she yelled to herself. Seeing Noah, she screamed. "Oh my God! Sean Connery is running the trial of the century! Can I get your autograph, Sean?"

"I'm not Sean Connery!" Noah said from the bench. The woman pulled out her cell phone and made a phone call.

"Oh my God! Betty, I'm inside! And Sean Connery – no, no wait – Martha Stewart – no, no, wait, it IS Sean Connery – and he's presiding over the trial of the century!"

Noah banged his gavel three times. "Martha Stewart? What is wrong with you people? Don't you recognize a real celebrity when you see one?"

"Well, Sean," the woman continued, pointing at Steve, "T-Bone is here. He's right there. I mean, you haven't made a decent movie in some time, and T-Bone's popping up all over the place these days -"

"I'm not Sean Connery, you idiot! Look, don't you people

realize that I saved your asses a long time ago?"

"Oh, boy, here we go," Julie said, "I've heard this story a thousand times. Better get comfortable. Next thing you know he's gonna be singing that stupid song. Again."

"The Lord told Noah," Noah started singing softly, "to build him an Arky, Arky, the Lord told Noah, to build him an Arky, Arky, build it out of gopher barky, barky…"

The young woman bounced around the courtroom, her phone to her ear. "Betty, Martha Stewart is going a little crazy! Wanna see?" She took the phone from her ear and snapped a photograph. "Check it out! Martha, you're now trending on Twitter!"

Noah banged his gavel on the podium 12 times and his face turned beet red. "LOOK, PEOPLE, Chris wanted to completely eradicate your planet the first time, but I talked her into letting me take eight people on a boat with a bunch of animals for a long freaking time, and it sucked, but you, as a race, were saved. I saved you because your planet just happens to have the best peanuts for making peanut butter, and because I know that humans know how to make the best peanut butter. I saved you. Now you pay me back by forgetting who I am?"

The courtroom was silent for about 3.7 seconds, and then the young woman spoke.

"Dude, okay, so you're not Sean Connery. Look, I'm sorry you're not a celebrity. Maybe, if you can sing, you can try out for 'American Idol' or 'American's Got Talent' or 'The X Factor' or 'The Voice,' or, maybe, if you have a video camera and a hotel room, you can make a sex tape. Or marry a Kardashian or something. Okay? So, chill out, dude. Everybody gets their fifteen minutes. This is America!" She held up her cellphone to take a selfie and giggled.

Jim stood up and approached the bench. "This is all fine and dandy, your honor, but the rain is getting louder, and we should really get this trial started and over with before we drown. My client," he said, pointing at Steve, "wishes to enter a plea of 'not guilty,' due to excessive peanut butter and banana sandwich consumption, and -"

"The trial *is* over with," Noah said.

"But, your honor," Jim said, his faced scrunched up like a child doubting his parent, "there's still the temporary insanity plea, then there's the part where we pick twelve people to judge my client, and then we throw the smartest of those twelve out and get twelve more, and -

"Ah, you really are a lawyer, aren't you?"

"The last one."

"Damn," Noah said. "That means he has to take you."

"Yes, it does, doesn't it?"

"Well, that solves the question of what do the animals eat."

"Wait, what?"

The butler entered the courtroom, dressed in in a black tuxedo, with a black shirt, black bowtie, and black top hat. In his hand, a tray of drinks and peanut butter and banana sandwiches, which he began to hand to everybody in the room.

"Please to meet you," he said with a sly grin, "hope you guess my name." He removed his top hat and his face turned fire red, just as a pair of red horns erupted from his head. He started to waltz out of the room, literally, but Noah came down from his bench and stood between him and the door.

"Oh, no you don't."

"I know who you are!" the young woman squealed. "Betty, Lucifer is here! Look!" She pointed her cell phone at the butler. "And he just did a wardrobe reveal!"

"Wait," Noah, said, turning to the young woman, "you recognize him, but you don't recognize me?"

"Oh, wait, wait, I think I do. You're Craig T. Nelson, of 'Coach' fame?"

"THAT DOES IT!" Noah yelled to the ceiling. "BRING ON THE RAIN!"

Thunder cracked outside the courtroom.

"Now you've done it," Julie said with a blank face.

"Done what?" Steve asked.

"Pissed him off," Julie said. Jane slid into the courtroom through the back door and sidled up to Steve.

"Sorry," he whispered to her.

"I know," she replied.

She kissed his cheek as he melted into her eyes and tingles enveloped his body. And something else enveloped his mind. Hip, Steve thought. No, that's not right. He pulled out his Big Dic and looked up a word.

"This mission is over!" Noah continued. "You humans are worse than I thought. How can you not recognize the man who saved your entire race?" He smiled and pointed to his face. The courtroom was quiet. "Well, now Chris can do whatever she wants with you. I'm not going to stop her this time. Let the rain come. Hard and fast. To hell with peanut butter. And you," he said to the butler, "until the water gets too high, you can have free reign of this planet."

"I already do," the butler said, his red face cracking, his grin as wide as the sky.

"I'm outta here," Noah said, and started towards the back door.

"Now wait a minute," Steve said, as Jane held his hand. "You can't just drown all these people. We need some more time to finish the mission, so we can save some of them and start again. As crazy as this place is – and it's easy to get sucked into that – there's something worth saving here. They really just need a warning shot. There is still -" He looked at Jane and then at his Big Dic. "Hope."

"Steve, you know so little," Noah said.

"I know that there are people here who, deep down inside, wait -" Steve stood up on the plywood soap box in the center of the room, shared a smile with Jane, and continued. "I know that there are people here who really do care for one another and for their planet. And I do know that, while appearing stupid on the outside at times, humans for the most part are intelligent on the inside. And I do know that there's a beauty to living on this planet that will only, in time, bring them back around. They're circular! You gotta give them a chance."

"Oh, brother," Noah said, shaking his head. "You don't know anything. They're going to drown."

"Not if I can help it. Stop the rain, Noah, or I'll kick your ass." Steve crouched down in his best martial arts pose; it was something he learned from Bruce Lee's Thursday afternoon martial arts classes.

"Oh, please," Noah said, sarcasm dripping from his words like maple syrup from a stack of pancakes. "Don't. Stop. Don't Stop." He pulled a pistol from his robe. "Haven't you learned anything? Look, Steve, don't make me shoot you. Please. And don't mess around with things you know nothing about. We sent you here on a mission, and you were too young to accomplish that mission. Too young and too stupid. Now it's over. You can go home. Okay? Home to your mommy where you're safe and you can't get into any more trouble. Let this work be done by qualified contractors or I'm going to kill you." A shot rang out and Noah slumped over. Steve looked in the direction of the shot and saw Jane with a pistol of her own. A smoking pistol.

"Jane!"

She lifted the barrel in the air and blew at it with her lips, as if she had just bagged a trophy elk. "Sometimes a gun *is* the only way to solve a problem."

"Dude," the young woman said.

"Dude," Jim said.

"Noah, are you okay?" Julie asked.

"Betty, did you see that?" the young woman asked her cell phone.

"Jane," Steve said, "you saved my life." He stared at her like a man stares at a woman who has just saved his life. Which she had. So the simile in this case was really a reality. "Even though I was a complete jerk to you."

"It's kind of funny isn't it?" Jane replied. "Wow – I have a sense of humor! I guess the pills DO work."

From the floor where Noah fell, a groan. A moan. A sigh. And then desperate words. "Steve, there's one thing I need to tell you."

"What?" Steve replied, hoping this wouldn't take long, because he hoped that he and Jane, after everything that had happened, were going to make lawn tonight. Wait, that wasn't right. He pulled out his Big Dic; make *love* tonight. Ah. That would be a lot more fun than making a lawn.

"Well, okay," Noah groaned from the floor. "Two things. Okay, actually, three things."

"Well, are you going to spit them out or do we need to do the Heimlich on you?" Steve asked.

"I don't think the Heimlich is going to get this bullet out of my chest."

"Well?" Steve asked. "Are you gonna tell me? I have a lawn to sow."

"Okay, first of all, you've been elected governor of California."

"But I wasn't even really running," Steve replied. "Wow. How does somebody with no experience get elected to public office like that?" He knew he was popular, but seriously?

"Steve?" Noah asked from the floor.

"Yes?"

"Can I finish?"

"Oh, sure. Sorry."

"Secondly, I just want you all to know that I have Thanatophobia. That's fear of dying."

"I think we all have that, honey – uh, Noah." Julie said.

"Honey?" Jim replied. "You – and Noah?"

"Well, yeah, I guess now that he's dying, I can let the cat out of the bag," Julie replied. "We've been having an affair. If I couldn't drive the damn boat, at least I could be with the celebrity who was most well known for driving the boat." She turned to Steve. "If you had completed your mission, you were next in line to drive the boat. Fucker."

From the floor, a moan. And "Honey?"

"Yes, dear?"

"Can I finish?"

"Oh – okay," she replied. "I guess it is your time to shine. Sorry. Go ahead."

"Steve, I have one more thing to say to you," Noah groaned from the floor, and the courtroom was quiet for a few seconds. "Steve, I am your father." He groaned again, his eyes rolled back in his head, and he took his last breath.

"Oh, shit," Jane said, "I killed your father."

"Dude," the young woman said.

"Dude," Jim said.

"Didn't see that coming," Julie replied. "I mean, I thought you were an orphan, Steve."

"Me, too," Steve replied. It was what he was always told.

"And Noah always said he didn't like kids," she continued. "Maybe he was talking about goats that whole time."

"Uh, hello?" Jim said.

"My father's dead," Steve said, his face a mass of glum. He, honestly, had seen his first meeting with his father going differently, somehow.

"I'm sorry, Steve," Jane said, and she gave Steve a strong hug.

"People?" Jim asked.

"What?" Julie, Jane, and Steve asked at the same time.

"It's raining pretty hard," Jim said. "Maybe we should think about getting out of here. Before it's too late."

A ringtone pierced the air of the courtroom, like an arrow piercing a balloon, and Steve put his cellphone up to his ear.

"Hellooooo? I'm fine, John. Yeah, I see that it's raining. What's going on?" Steve listened to his phone intently for a moment. "The boat is ready? Well, isn't that scrumpdillyumptious?"

"I think the word you're looking for 'fortuitous,'" Jane quietly said to him.

"Oh," Steve said, "Isn't that fortuitous?" He put the phone back up to his ear. "Yeah, John, we'll be over shortly. Start it up."

"The boat is ready?" Jim asked.

"Yeah, my fans and sponsors finished it for John."

Kyle Carpenter motioned to her camera man and spoke to the camera. "The boat is ready! This is Kyle Carpenter, 6:00 news, signing off, for the last time! I'm on the list, so I'm outta here!" She started running towards the back door.

"You're on the list?" Jim asked.

She stopped running, turned back to Jim, winked, and said, "I'm merely saying that it's fortuitous that every other news anchor on the planet disappeared." She turned and ran out the back door of the courtroom, followed by the young woman on the cell phone.

"Jane?" Steve said.

"Steve?" Jane replied.

"Thanks to my fans and the Really Big Burger Company, the boat's ready."

"So I suppose that means you're leaving?"

"Yeah. I mean, I have a job to do. A new job. The human race must survive, and I want to be a part of that. They're not so bad, you know. You showed me that." It was true. He learned more about human nature from Jane's lectures than from actual humans themselves, a thought that gave him pause.

Until Jane stared deep into his eyes. "I'm proud of you, Steve."

"Uh," Jim interrupted, "can I go on your boat?"

"Well," Steve replied, not looking at Jim, "we do need something for the animals to eat." He turned to Jim. "That's a joke, man!

Go get on the boat!" Jim turned and ran out the back door of the courtroom. "Jane?"

"Steve?"

"Will you have sex with me sometime?"

"Do you mean coffee?"

"No, I mean sex. We're past the coffee part. And that boat's going to get awfully lonely."

"I'll have sex with you forty times in forty days."

"And then sandwiches and naps?"

"You catch on quickly. Let's go." She grabbed his hand and the two of them ran out the back door of the courtroom.

Julie and the butler were the only two left standing in the courtroom; loud thunder continued outside with increasing frequency, restless, like a stadium full of people anticipating the headlining act taking the stage.

"Well, I guess it's all mine now," the butler said, looking up to the sky, his red arms outstretched. He turned to Julie. "You wanna help me get this party started?"

"What are you going to do?"

"Well, I've been building my own boat, in the other harbor. It's a bit smaller than Steve's boat, but it'll hold the best of the worst that humanity has to offer. I figure I'll go to Las Vegas and round up all the best sinners around, load the boat up with booze and smokes and slot machines, and we'll go on a little trip. Then, when the waters subside, there'll be yin to Steve's yang. Checks and balances. Take the good with the bad. It's the only way all of this works."

"Oh," Julie replied with a sigh as she turned away and stifled a sob.

"And I need a driver."

"Me?" She wiped her face on her arm and turned back around.

"What do you think?"

"Sign me up, Captain Stubing," Julie said, saluting with her right hand.

"What?"

"Nevermind, let's just go."

Julie grabbed the hand of the Demon Formerly Known As Butler and ran out the back door as the courtroom strained against the oncoming storm and the world came to an end.

Again.

THE END ?

FROM THE AUTHOR

Estes Park, CO – 2018

I'm at my annual writer's retreat, sitting on the front porch of the lovely Stanley Hotel, overlooking the gorgeous Rocky Mountains, thinking about the randomness of inspiration…

It was a dark and stormy night at my house in Denver a while back and, amidst the pitter-patter of the rain hitting the roof and the jarring bursts of thunder, the doorbell rang.

And inspiration took over.

And "Flood" was born.

At the time I was writing pieces for the stage as a member of a rogue band of playwrights and actors who called ourselves "Bootstrap Productions." We had a theater space that we shared with a bigger, much less rogue-y theater group, so we were able to produce our own shows on the nights they weren't using the space. Which means the pieces we were writing would see the stage on Tuesdays and Wednesday nights, and "Flood" was one of those pieces.

Some time later, I turned to fiction and, after "American Badass" and its sequel "50 Shades of Brain," I was looking for the next spark, the next inspiration. As I sat in my office one night with a nice glass of bourbon and considered my options, the script for "Flood" jumped out and demanded that I take it, a work that was all dialog, and turn it into a full-blown novel. I was inspired, and it sounded easy.

It wasn't.

But it was a helluva lot of fun. And, really, isn't that what it's all about?

ACKNOWLEDGMENTS

Thanks to:

—The members of Bootstrap Productions and Colorado Dramatists, past and present, for creating the space to play with ideas. "Flood" came from that space.

—The good people in The Room 217 Writers Group for the shop talk, the camaraderie, and the Stanley Hotel retreats. You shine.

—My writing group for reading my garbage and helping me turn it into something slightly less garbage-y.

—Anthony Reynoso for helping with a lot of the animal factoids in the book. That guy's pretty smart.

—My family for letting me disappear occasionally so I can feed my muse.

—Wooden Stake Press for continuing to support my flights of flatulence. Sorry, fancy. Flights of fancy.

—And you, dear reader, for diving in and giving fiction a

chance. I hope this book is a helluva lot of fun for you. Because really, isn't that what it's all about?

ABOUT THE AUTHOR

JEFF CHACON is the author of *American Badass*, a Vegas Zom-Com (a genre Jeff made up) novel. He is also the author of its sequel *50 Shades of Brain* and co-author of the cult comedy classic *E-Male: of mouse and men*. He has appeared on theater and rock and roll stages all over Colorado and California in several productions and bands you've never heard of. He lives with his wife and kids in Denver.

ABOUT THE PRESS

Wooden Stake Press LLC publishes whatever strikes our fancy. Visit us on the web at www.woodenstakepress.com.

www.ingramcontent.com/pod-product-compliance
Lightning Source LLC
Chambersburg PA
CBHW030342180626
46812CB00007B/2728